KIKI SW[...]

PRESENTS

CHEAPER to KEEP HER

PART 4

AMERICA'S MOST WANTED

A NOVEL

UNIQUE

This is a work of fiction. All of the characters, organizations, and events portrayed in this novel are either products of the author's imagination or are used fictitiously.

Publisher's address:

K.S. Publications
P.O. Box 68878
Virginia Beach, VA 23471

Website: www.kikiswinson.net
Email: KS.publications@yahoo.com

ISBN-13: 978-0984529049
ISBN-10: 0984529047

First Edition: January 2013

10 9 8 7 6 5 4 3 2 1

Editors: J.Wooden & Letitia Carrington
Interior & Cover Design: Davida Baldwin (OddBalldsgn.com)
Cover Photo: Davida Baldwin

Printed in the United States of America

KS Publications
www.kikiswinson.net

Don't Miss Out On These Other Titles:

Wifey – (Series)
I'm Still Wifey
Life After Wifey
Still Wifey Material
Wifey 4-Life
Wife Extraordinaire (New Wifey series)
Wife Extraordinaire Returns (part 2)
Wife Extraordinaire Reloaded (part 3)
The Candy Shop – (Series)
Still Candy Shopping
A Sticky Situation
Sleeping with the Enemy (with Wahida Clark)
Heist (with De'nesha Diamond)
Life Styles of the Rich and Shameless (with Noire)
Playing Dirty
Notorious
New York's Finest – (Series)
Internationally Known: New York's Finest part 2
Cheaper to Keep Her part 1 – (Series)
Cheaper to Keep Her part 2: The Saga Continues
Cheaper to Keep Her part 3: More Money More Problems
Green Eye Bandit (part 1)

EPILOGUE:

(PREVIOUSLY PRINTED IN CHEAPER TO KEEP HER PART 3)

FINALLY GETTING SOME CLOSURE

Agent Morris and I searched through the rubble and finally saw Agent Wise. The devastating part about finding her was the fact that she was dead. She had gotten ran over by the car. We could only see part of her face and it was saturated with her blood. Luckily she was facing the opposite direction because her eyes were open, so I didn't think I'd be able to handle looking at her head on.

Agent Morris immediately radioed Agent Sean because he lost his cell phone amongst the debris. While he communicated with Sean, I ran back into my bedroom to get my things because I knew it would be a matter of minutes before we got out of here. "We're about two hundred feet away from you, so stay put." I heard Sean tell Agent Morris.

"Copy that." Agent Morris replied. Soon he was down on my heels. "Come on, we got to get out of here." he said.

I grabbed my things I had packed earlier and followed Agent Morris to the front door. Several seconds later,

Agent Sean appeared with five other agents. It was one female and four men. All of them including Sean were dressed in military issued fatigue gear, bulletproof vests inscribed with "FBI" on them and the heaviest, most deadly artillery one man could carry in their arms. They looked like they were ready for war.

Sean grabbed me by my arm. "Come on, let's get you out of here."

I swear, this was the first time that I can truly say that I was happy to see his ass. And I was convinced that he would risk his life to save mine. He was geared up and ready to serve and protect.

A few of the neighbors stood outside while Sean and two other agents escorted me to the car. Local police even joined the party. "We're taking you somewhere safe." he told me.

"Okay," I replied.

When Sean helped me into the exact same black Suburban that followed Bishop and I down the New Jersey Turnpike, I shook my head. Who would've thought that I'd be traveling in it after Bishop noticed it on the turnpike and it was parked a couple of blocks from the house he shared with Keisha? Strange things intend to always happen.

While I sat inside of the truck, both of the agents guarded the truck from the outside. The windows were tinted so no one was able to see what position I was sitting in. "Do you have everything you need?" he asked me.

"Yeah," I said.

"Well, hold tight and I'll be right back."

"Can you please hurry up? 'Cause I can't stand to be out here another minute."

"Don't worry, I'll be right back." He assured me and then he ran back towards the apartment.

I looked around the surrounding area and saw how most of the neighbors were migrating towards my apartment to see what all of the commotion was. I also watched as Sean, several police officers, and the other agents were inspecting the old car that smashed in the wall of my living room. Moments later, I watched as the city tow truck service had arrived on the scene. Agent Sean said a few words to the tow truck driver and then he walked away from the truck. From that point, the tow truck driver proceeded to pull the car back out of my living room.

Before he was able to remove the car from the apartment, Sean and four police officers and the other two agents had to lift the car up so the tow truck driver wouldn't pull Agent Wise's body with it. And only after they struggled for ten minutes, the car was finally removed.

Immediately after Agent Wise's body was attainable, a coroner had arrived, bagged up her body and then they took her away. I didn't know her, but watching the coroner take her body away was a sad thing to see because I could've very well taken her place. I just hoped that she didn't have any kids. It would be a sad day if she did.

A few more minutes passed but it seemed like time stood still. The crowd outside of my apartment grew larger by the minute. The agents and the police used yellow crime tape to secure the crime scene. It felt like I was watching an episode of CSI. But with the horrific scenes of that crime drama, I wasn't ready when Sean came back to the truck with some more grim news.

After he climbed in the back seat where I was, he closed the door and said, "We just found Bria's body in the trunk of that car. And it looks like she's been dead at least two days."

Hearing the words, Bria's body, took a few minutes before it registered in my mind. And when it finally did, I was completely taken aback. But for some reason I needed to know more. "Was she shot?"

"She was wearing a blindfold and it definitely appears that she died from a gunshot wound to the head. So whoever shot her did it execution style."

"Whatcha' mean who ever did it? We both know that Bishop did that shit! That crazy motherfucker killed his own fucking sister. Now how fucked up is that. I swear, I hope y'all give that son of a bitch the death penalty when you catch his ass."

"Listen, we're gonna need you to help bring this joker down. Now Keisha has already agreed to help, and since you're already on board we need to get you out of here right now and take you somewhere safe until we take him into custody." Sean said.

"Well, I'm ready." I assured him.

"So, you know, we're taking you to a Witness Protection Program."

"But, I don't wanna go into Witness Protection. I already told Agent Morris, I wasn't feeling that. People that are snitching go into that program and I'm not that kind of person. I was forced to help y'all. And look where it got me."

"Okay listen, not all snitches go into that program. That program is for your protection. It's government funded, so we can use all the resources to make sure nothing happens to you."

I sat there with my arms folded and thought about what other options I had. And I came up with absolutely nothing. I did have Bishop's dope and sixty-eight thousand dollars. So, after all this mess is over with, I'd be well equipped to go on my merry way.

Once I was able to ponder on this situation I finally told Sean I'd go to the program but I made him promise that as soon as Bishop was locked up, I'd be free to go. He agreed and then we shook on it. But before he got back out of the truck he looked at me and said, "I'm glad you agreed to get protection because when we looked in the trunk and saw the garbage bag, it had a note taped to it that said, "Lynise this will be you next."

Shaking with fear, I said, "Oh my God! Are you for real?"

"Yes, I am. And that's why it's important for you to get into the program so what happened to her won't happen to you."

"Look, I've heard enough. Can somebody get me out of here right now?" I asked nervously.

"I'm gonna get Agent Pax and Agent Morris to transport you to a safe location in just a minute." he replied.

After he gave me the rundown, he slid back out of the truck and pulled Agent Morris to the side. Seconds later, I saw Agent Morris coming towards me so I knew I was about to be out of this place.

It's real in the field!

Agent Morris got on the passenger side of the truck while Agent Pax drove. It felt good to be getting away from the apartment but these dumb ass cats thought I was going to be around for the long haul. No sir! Not me! I swear after all this shit is over, I'm getting missing in action. And once I get rid of the dope, I should have enough money to last me as long as I lived modestly and stayed underneath the radar. For now, I intended to keep my money and my plans a mystery. It's about Lynise and Lynise only.

"Where exactly are you guys taking me?" I asked. I figured since I was going in hiding; why not find out where they were taking me. I mean, it was my life that was on the line and I felt like whom better to look after it but me.

"We're taking you to a secured location called the safe house." Agent Morris answered.

"Is that like a house y'all got hidden in the woods or something?"

"I see you watch a lot of TV." Agent Morris commented.

"Yeah, I love the show CSI and In Plain Sight." I replied and then I turned my attention to the high-rise buildings as we passed them. "How faraway is this place? Because it'll be a bummer if we gotta drive more than thirty miles."

"You shouldn't be worried about where we're taking you or how long it'll take us to get you there. Everything we do is confidential. But I will say that the place is safe and secured. And no one will be able to find it."

"Can you at least tell me if y'all are taking me out of the state?" I continued to probe.

"No. You're staying within the city limits. And once Bishop is picked up and prosecuted, then you'll be able to leave and go wherever you want," he answered.

Agent Morris kept giving me the runaround about where they were taking me so I left the whole thing alone. I wasn't the type of chick that begged anyone. No way. He got me confused with somebody else.

During the rest of the drive the agents talked amongst themselves so I went into thought mode. I couldn't help but wonder where they were going to house me and how long I was going to be there. Finding out this information would help me figure out how to make my escape plan and how long I would need to come up with one.

Finally after a thirty-five minute drive, Agent Morris told Agent Pax he had to use the bathroom. "Pull over to the Exxon gas station so I can use the bathroom." he said.

"Yeah, I gotta take a leak myself." Agent Pax told him.

"Well, I'll go first and when I get back, I'll stay here and let you go." Agent Morris insisted.

"Let's do it." Agent Pax said and then he stopped and parked the SUV next to one of the gas pumps.

I sat in the backseat and watched Agent Morris walk to the men's restroom, which was inside of the station. The sun was shining bright and it seemed as though everybody was outside. I looked around to my left and saw a cute little Volkswagon Passat. It was white in color and it looked like it had just been driven off the showroom floor. The chick behind the wheel parked it at the gas pump next to ours. And when she got out of the car, I immediately knew that she was a stone cold gold digger. To sum up how she looked, she looked like she was Hispanic and black. Her hair was very long, but she wore it up in a ponytail. And she definitely had the body of a video vixen, minus the butt pads. I watched her as she removed a McDonald's bag and a drink cup from her car and threw it into the trashcan next to her pump.

When Agent Morris came back outside this young lady caught his eye. He got her attention by saying something to her and after she looked up, she smiled and stopped everything she was doing. I watched them as they walked towards each other. I made a comment to Agent Pax about Agent Morris flirting with the woman. "Check out Agent Morris flirting with that young Spanish hottie." I commented.

"Where?" Agent Pax asked.

"To your left." I replied.

Agent Pax turned to his left and saw Agent Morris talking with the woman. "He's not flirting with her. That's Chrissy. She's one of our linguist specialists." Agent Pax said.

"Did you say Chrissy?" I said aloud, because for some reason that name rung out to me.

"Yeah, why you know her?" Agent Pax asked me.

Before I answered him I thought back to the time I spoke with a Chrissy from Bishop's phone. And I remembered Bishop talking to Monty about a Chrissy. But could this be the same Chrissy? "Nah, I don't know her. But I do know somebody with the same name." I finally replied.

"We all do." Agent Pax commented.

"So, what exactly does she do?" I wanted to know.

"She's the best translator in our office."

"Oh really?"

"Yes, she speaks like four or five different languages."

"Wow! That's hot!"

Minutes later, Agent Morris decided to join us. But instead of climbing back into the SUV on the passenger side, he walked up to the driver side with Chrissy in tow. Agent Pax rolled down his window. "What are you doing on this side of town?"

"My mom lives near here so I decided to come out here to visit." she told him.

I swear, when she started talking I nearly pissed in my pants. This was the exact same chick I talked to on Bishop's cell phone. She had the same fucking squeaky voice. But how was it that she was involved with Agent Morris? I was completely at a loss for words. I was literally confused and had no idea what to do.

"Today is definitely a nice day to take a drive." Agent Pax assured her.

"Tell me about it," she commented. And then she said, "So, where are you guys on your way to?" she wanted to know.

But before either one of them could respond to her I interjected by saying, "Don't tell her! She's working for Bishop."

Agent Pax turned completely around in his seat to get a good look at me while Agent Morris peaked his head into the driver side window. And when Agent Morris opened his mouth to say something to me, both agents got their heads blown off. Agent Morris and Agent Pax's brains where splattered all over the front seat, the windshield and some of their blood and pieces of body tissue plopped on me as well. I was in complete shock. And I screamed as loud as I could.

Now after she took both of these men out, she pulled on the backdoor handle and tried to open it. Lucky for me, it was locked. "Somebody help me!" I screamed.

I saw at least five people near their cars but no one wanted to come near the truck. I did see this lady get on her cell phone, so I assumed she was calling the police.

"Somebody please help me! She's trying to kill me!" I continued to scream. I needed some fucking help. I figured that if these people weren't going to risk their lives to save mine, then they'd at least call the cops for me.

After three failed attempts to open both back doors, Chrissy tried to shoot the windows out but she couldn't get them to budge. And when she finally figured out that they were bullet proofed she stuck her gun inside the driver side window and aimed it at me. She pulled the trigger and I ducked down behind the seat but that didn't prevent me from getting hit. The bullet went right through my left shoulder. The feeling of that bullet burning through my skin was unbearable. And I knew that if she got the chance to shoot me again, I wasn't going to make it. But thank God, she emptied out the clip on both agents and the windows, because when she finally got to me, she only had one bullet left.

With the combination of frustration and hearing the police blaring their sirens, Chrissy hopped back into her car and sped off. I swear, I never felt so relieved.

Minutes after the cops and the paramedics arrived, I was carried out of the truck and placed on a stretcher. And right before they put me into the ambulance, I made sure they grabbed my purse and laid it beside me. I was in very bad shape but that didn't alter my judgment in any way. I had some very valuable possessions stashed away inside of it and there was no way I was going to compromise it.

Finally arriving at the hospital, the paramedics pulled up to the emergency dock. And when they rolled me out the back of the ambulance, they placed the stretcher on the ground and that's when I got a strange feeling that someone was watching me.

So, while they rolled me towards the entryway, I lifted my head as much as I could and when I looked towards the parking lot, I saw this man who looked just like Bishop sitting behind the wheel of a parked car. My heart did summersaults. But at the same time, I wondered if I was seeing things. So, I closed my eyes and when I opened them back up, I took a second look but the car was gone. Now was my mind really playing tricks on me? Or was Bishop lurking out there and waiting patiently for the perfect time to take me out? I couldn't answer the first question but I knew he wanted me dead. And he wouldn't stop at nothing until it was done.

Thank God I'm still alive!

WHY ME?

This morning marked my third day in this shithole of a hospital. Not only was the accommodations whack, the food sucked too and I wanted out of here. While I was laid up in the hospital, Agent Foster had two agents posted outside my room standing guard. Having me to only assist them in their investigation against Bishop and his crew went out the window after I witnessed Chrissy execute Agents Morris and Pax. I was officially a government witness and I hated it.

Agent Foster gave my new agents strict orders to protect me at all cost. That meant it was controlled traffic coming in and going out of my room. My plan of getting the hell out of Newark and going to another state to start over was a distant memory. Before he left my room, Sean and I had a one-on-one chat about how we planned to proceed from here.

"How are you feeling?" he started off. He acted like he was truly concerned for my wellbeing.

I sighed. "Like shit!" I replied full of exasperation.

"You shouldn't be in here much longer," he stated.

"So what's gonna happen next?" I asked him. I needed some answers. Sean and I crossed paths during his investigation of Bishop and his sister, Bria. After Bria went missing or shall I say, got killed, my life collapsed into a downward spiral. I thought I was coming to New Jersey to start a new life with Bishop, but that dream went up in smoke after all the drama unfolded between his bitch Keisha and I. And to make matters worse, after he found out about I was assisting Agent Sean Foster with his investigation, everything Bishop and I had built fell apart.

It seemed as if I went from one hellhole to the next. I figured the only way I'd come out of this mess in one piece was if I teamed up with God and let him handle it. I've always had a problem with asking God to help me with certain situations. It just seemed like God took His sweet time in making things happen, so I'd take it upon myself to work the situation out on my own. *Poor little me!* I never knew how to stop interfering with God's work. I figured now would be a perfect time to do so since I had no other options.

"After the hospital discharges you," Agent Foster began. "I plan to have you stay in one of our safe houses. That way we can monitor you twenty-four hours a day until we hand you over to the US Marshals."

"I'm not going with no US Marshals. I'm staying with you until all this mess is over." I spat. The thought of putting my life in the hands of some people I didn't know, made me sick to my stomach.

"I'm sorry Lynise, but that's the way things have to be. I didn't make up the rules. But I have to follow them." He continued to explain to me.

I rolled my eyes. Well, how long do you plan on having me in this safe house?" I asked with much attitude.

"Hopefully, not long." That answer was ominous so I wanted to know more.

"And approximately how long is not long in your FBI manual?"

"One to two weeks max."

"Are you fucking kidding me? I can't be cooped up in a safe house that long. I've got shit I've got to do," I protested. One to two weeks seemed like forever in my mind. "Who's gonna be there with me?"

"Me and a couple of agents will rotate shifts."

"But what if I want you there with me the entire time?" I responded. "I mean, I know you more so than I know them." Truth be told, I had feelings for this guy. I liked him from the first day I laid eyes on him. But after he told me he was a fucking Federal agent working with Bishop's sister Bria up until the time she went missing, put a sour taste in my mouth. I was a street chick. And street chicks weren't supposed to think cops as being sexy. This type of nonsense was going against the grain, so to speak. So I buried the feelings I had until now.

In a weird kind of way, Agent Foster was the kind of guy I needed in my life. He was someone who was legit and he wasn't into a lot of bullshit. Living a life full of turmoil was what I had going on and I didn't know how to navigate out of it. As much as I thought I wanted to get out, I had to be real with myself. My heart was drawn to niggas living the thug life. Living on the edge was an act of courage and that did something to me. So whether I wanted to be with Agent Foster or the next street cat, I knew I had to make a choice.

"Look, I'll tell you what, I'll talk with my supervisor and see what I can do," he said to me.

"Just tell 'em I only feel safe around you and if they want me to help get Bishop's ass and tell them what I know about his sister's death and the death of the other agents, then they gotta give me you."

Agent Foster smiled. "You drive a hard bargain."

"I'm sure it seems that way. But Bishop is out to get me and I feel like you're the only one who could protect me. So, am I wrong for that?"

"Of course not."

"All right then," I commented.

After I pleaded my case with Agent Foster, he told me he had to take care of a few things back at the office that concerned the four agents that died after the shooting and the car incident involving a car that knocked down the wall in my apartment. I watched him closely. From the way he licked his lips to the way he walked, Agent Foster had it going on in my mind. He was more handsome today than he had ever been. If I wasn't bandaged up and hooked to this IV, I'd have this nigga jump in bed with me. There was no doubt in my mind that he was packing a ton. I was a good judge when it came to measuring a nigga's dick through his pants and I saw a bulge that wouldn't wait. Boy, I'd have a field day with this guy. I'd even try to get pregnant, without his knowledge of course. That's just how fly he was. Every time he talked and made hand gestures, he reminded me of Jamie Foxx. And everybody knew how fly Jamie Foxx was. Well, that was how I saw Agent Sean Foster.

Everything was running smoothly until some random ass doctor walked into the room acting like he was God. I was mad as hell when he came in and interrupted our flow. When he introduced himself and told me he was the doctor on duty I became more annoyed. This idiot wasn't even the doctor that operated on me. So why was he wasting my fucking time?

"How are you feeling?" the Indian doctor asked me. When I heard his accent I became even more irritated. I couldn't hardly understand shit he was saying so I was ready for him to haul ass immediately.

"I'm going to go so you can talk to the doctor," Agent Foster said and then he excused himself. I was furious with the doctor for coming in my room and interrupting me and Agent Foster.

"Not too good," I replied with much attitude. But I really wanted to say something else. I mean, he saw me laid up in the fucking hospital bed trying to heal from a gunshot wound, so how else would I feel? In all fairness he needed to take his ass down the hall and check on some of the other patients. Someone he'd operated on would be ideal for him.

"Well, don't worry. You will be fine," he commented as he looked at my chart. After he scribbled a few words on the paper, he told me he'd check on me later, which I knew was a lie. Lying to patients to make themselves' look good was customary for doctors.

"Can you tell me when I'm getting out of here?" I managed to blurt out.

"Very soon," he replied, which in my mind meant that he really didn't know. It didn't surprise me the way he brushed me off. I was in a hospital in the heart of Newark, New Jersey and I heard the medical services here sucked. Medical service provided in any hospital in an urban area was horrible because of state funding, so I figured since I wasn't dying, then I would be fine just like he said.

On his way out of my room, I gritted my teeth and turned my attention towards the TV. There wasn't anything on worth watching, but it was more entertaining than listening to that bootleg ass doctor.

I tried to get into *Celebrity Apprentice,* the reality show, but my mind wouldn't let me. I swear, I couldn't take my mind off Bishop and the fact that he sent Chrissy out to hunt me down and take me the fuck out. Who would've thought that he had an inside connection with a special agent? When I searched through Bishop's phone that night and called her number back, I never would've thought in a million years that I was talking to an agent. That ho really pulled the wool over my eyes. And so had Bishop.

The whole time I thought she was another one of his fuck partners trying to steal my spot. Instead, that cold-hearted bitch was an assassin on a mission. I thank God for His protection, because those two federal agents dropped the ball while they were transporting me. We never should have stopped at the gas station. But since they did, I was shot while their lives were taken. Talk about getting the short end of the stick.

Aside from Chrissy, I realized I was learning more and more about Bishop. He was well connected and when he had his mind fixed on something, he wouldn't stop at nothing until it was done. I had witnessed what he'd done to other people but I never would have thought he'd turn on me. I just hoped that I'd be able to slip through the cracks before he got a chance to close in on me. The only good thing that weighed in my favor was the fact that I wasn't the only person on his shit list. His main lady Keisha was at the top of his hit list. So if I used that to my advantage, I may come out in the clear. I guess, time would tell though.

During the next several hours, nurses and certified nursing assistants paraded in and out of my room and I wanted them to stop. I pulled one of the CNAs to the side and asked her a few questions. She was a young, short, black chick with a head full of blonde and black hair extensions. When she opened her mouth to speak, I knew she was straight from the hood. She put the "G" in ghetto. No pun intended.

"Is there any way I could request for all of the nurses to stop from coming in here for a while?" I asked. "All of this running in and out is preventing me from sleeping and I am about to go crazy." I complained. Those bitches were plucking my damn nerves and I wanted it to stop.

She smiled. "It's hospital policy to check on da patients around da clock. Girl, if da doctor found out we ain't been in here to check your vitals, our butts will be on the chopping block and I can't lose my job. It's bad enough dat I don't get no child support from my baby daddies, so you know I gotta follow da rules."

"How long have you been working here?" I wondered aloud.

"About two months now. The state made me go to school in order to still get my benefits, so here I am."

"Do what you gotta' do," I told her. "Is it still two agents standing outside my door?"

"It's only one now. I heard the other one went down to the cafeteria to get something to eat. Why you ask?"

"No reason really."

"So, are you really a government witness, like they say?" she began to probe while she took my blood pressure.

"If that's what you want to call it."

"Did they tell you how long you're supposed to be here?"

"Not yet. But I shouldn't be here too much longer."

The CNA chuckled. "You aren't from 'round here are you?"

"No, I'm not. But how did you guess?"

"You have a country accent."

"I'm from Virginia."

"What part?"

"Virginia Beach."

"Really? Is Virginia Beach as nice as everybody says it is?"

"Not to me, but I'm sure someone else would say differently," I commented while I watched her scribble something on my chart.

"Can you give me a number from one to ten describing your level of pain, ten being the highest?"

"I'm like a seven right now," I told her.

"Okay, well, I'm gonna give you another five mil of codeine through your IV," she told me.

The CNA was right, she had a job to do, especially if she had babies to take care of. I was cool with that. But, another nurse had just given me a dose of codeine a little over an hour ago, so I couldn't figure out why she wanted to give me some. Codeine was strong and it would send me into a deep sleep. But that's not what I wanted right now. I wanted to be alert and aware of my surroundings. Bishop was a very aggressive man and if he was given another chance to murder me, I knew he'd take it.

The young CNA continued to talk to me and ask me a bunch of unnecessary questions while she prepared the syringe to inject me with the liquid solution she called codeine. I looked at the bottle she was using. It didn't look like it came from a hospital pharmacy, even a ghetto hospital pharmacy so I became a little puzzled. The label on the bottle of the clear liquid looked old and part of the label was scraped off. Plus, the ink on the faded label was barely visible and that raised a huge, red flag for me. Something definitely wasn't right about this shit, so I politely pulled my arm back from her.

"Are you sure that's codeine?" I questioned her. "That shit you got in that bottle doesn't look like you got it from this hospital."

She tried to grab my arm back. "Give me your damn arm!" she barked. And that's when I knew that this bitch was a fucking fraud. What was even worse was that she was here to hurt me. Or better yet, kill me.

She wrestled with me to get my arm back into her grasp. "Somebody help! She's trying to kill me!" I screamed. My voice cracked a few times because of my dry mouth. At one point she tried to cover my mouth with one hand while she held onto the liquid filled syringe in the other. I tried to bite a plug out of her hand but she wouldn't let my mouth get close enough. I was recovering from a gunshot wound, so I had hardly any energy left to fight this chick off me. I knew I had to react quickly or my black ass would be dead, so I reached down by my left thigh to press the nurse call button. But she snatched it away from me.

"Shut up bitch and take it like a woman," she growled. Her face looked menacing all of a sudden. She was after blood and I was her target.

"Please help me! She's trying to kill me!" I screamed once more. This time my pitch was loud and clear. And in the blink of an eye, one of the agents standing guard outside my room burst into my room. I had never been so happy to see a man wearing a badge.

Once he realized what this crazy ass woman was doing he pulled his pistol from his holster and pointed it in her direction. "This is the FBI, release the patient right now or I will shoot!" he boomed. His voice ricocheted off every wall in my room. It was like music to my ears. Unfortunately for me, his words didn't penetrate her at all. She was adamant about shooting me up with whatever she had in that syringe no matter who was around. I realized that immediately after she held the needle against my neck. The tip of the needle was pinching my neck. I figured if I moved one inch, I'd be in trouble. She was definitely on a mission. And that mission was to take me out.

"Get back or I'll kill her!" she demanded after she jumped directly behind the head board of the hospital bed, using me as a shield.

"Please let me go," I begged as I tried to loosen the grip from around my neck.

"Nah bitch, you're gonna die!" she threatened me once again.

At this point, I knew this chick wasn't going to let me go. It didn't matter to her that the agent had just threatened to shoot her. Her mind had already been made up that she was going to kill me and no one was going to stop her.

I had no idea who this woman was but I knew she had heart. It took balls to come into a hospital surrounded by cops to murder a government witness. She had to know that she'd be signing her death certificate if she got caught. But then I realized the affect Bishop had on women and summed it up that she either had huge balls or that the bitch being a total nut job.

"Ma'am, I know you don't want to die. So, please put the needle down." He reasoned. He made it pretty obvious that he wasn't going anywhere and that it would be in her best interest to give herself up. But she wasn't going for the old banana in the tail pipe scenario; she was confident that she could hold her ground and do what she came in my room to do.

"Fuck that! If you don't get back I'm gonna kill her." She roared.

Seconds later, two shots were fired. I turned my face when I heard the explosion. Blood splattered against my face and body after the bullet penetrated her whole chest area. It literally just exploded on impact. And without another moments notice, her lifeless body collapsed onto the floor.

REALITY

I was still in shock after everything I had just went through. This was the third attempt on my life. So there was no denying it that Bishop wanted my black ass dead! That stupid ass bitch he hired had a death wish and the agent on guard granted her that wish.

"Goddammit, I want a list of all the doctors and nurses who will be attending to our witness," I heard Agent Foster say to a hospital administrator. "Plus, I don't want any more damn CNAs on the list, only doctors and nurses."

I was moved into a new room after the drama that unfolded in my old hospital room. Still, my room was chaotic. I was in a bigger room on the same floor. It had only been an hour since another one of Bishop's flunkies tried to take me out. Regardless of how big the room was, I still couldn't believe I had damn near twenty people in my room. I was sitting in a recliner chair that sat next to my bed. Agent Foster was talking to a female hospital administrator who had four or five medical personnel waiting to get me checked out.

I shook my head at all of the foolish drama.

I should have been shitting in my pants, but I was too tired and too fed up to be scared shitless. Don't get me wrong, I didn't want to die but if you've been knocked around as many times as I have, then you'd be sick and tired too. And if you'd look closely, I hadn't done anything wrong to warrant this behavior from Bishop. Okay granted, I never should've talked to Agent Foster. But he came at me first. And besides that, his sister Bria and his main chick Keisha sold him out first. So, why am I being stalked like this? Where is the sanity in all of this bullshit? I thank God I wasn't fighting this bastard alone. After watching Agent Foster rip the hospital staff a new asshole, I felt an even more intimate connection to him. It seemed like the louder he got the more attractive he became. In fact, I can honestly say that I was somewhat falling in love with him. The anger I heard in his voice spoke volumes. And it felt good to see that someone still cared about me. Agent Foster was definitely the man. And he made sure everyone knew it. After he praised my new, black hero named Agent Scott Rome for saving my life, he ordered the doctor to give me a thorough body exam to see if I had suffered more injuries and then he had the nurse take me into the bathroom and clean me up. He double checked their IDs and made sure at least five other hospital staff members could vouch for the doctor and nurse as well as the security officers.

"How are you feeling?" Agent Foster asked me.

"I'm a little shaken up but I'm fine for the most part." I told him. But what I really wanted to tell him was that I'd feel much better if he held me in his arms. It's been a minute since Bishop last held me, so I was overdo in the affection department.

"Well you'll feel even better after you settle down in this room." he expressed.

I looked around the new room I was in and took a quick survey of it. There was nothing spectacular about it. It looked just like the other room I was in. The only difference was that I was in a different part of the hospital. So, how in the hell was this room going to make me feel any better. In all honesty, Agent Foster was blowing smoke up my ass. I say, later with the bullshit and get me out of this hospital altogether. I've had enough of all the bootleg ass babysitters that were assigned to watch my back. Every single one of them allowed harm to come my way. Thank God for my sense of direction because I would've been dead a long time ago if I didn't.

After Agent Foster talked me too death about these lame ass accommodations he pulled Agent Rome to the side to speak with him in private. They stood near the door of my room and spoke just above a whisper.

I watched Agent Foster and Agent Rome's body language since I couldn't hear what they were saying. And from where I was sitting, it seemed like Agent Foster wasn't too happy about certain things Agent Rome had brought to his attention. "Just keep an eye on her and if it's true than we're gonna have to do things our way." Agent Foster said and then he shook his head like he was disgusted.

Immediately after their chat, Agent Rome excused himself and assured both Agent Foster and I that he'd be outside if we needed him. “Alright, but stay close.” Agent Foster replied and then he turned his focus towards me.

By this time, I had laid my head back against the pillow on my bed while my eyes stared at the ceiling. And all I could think about was how fucked up my life had become. I was on a rollercoaster ride going nowhere fast. The worse part about it was that I wanted out of this predicament but I knew that was a long shot. I was buried too deep. And if I wanted to come out of this alive, I knew I'd have to make a few vital decisions.

As soon as Agent Rome closed the door, Agent Foster sat at the end of my bed and said, “Pretty soon we're gonna have to move you out of here and take you to a more secured location.”

“When will that be?”

“I'm waiting to get the green light now. So, whenever it comes, that's when we're gonna bail out of here.”

“Is that what you and Agent Rome were talking about over by the door?” I asked.

“No. He and I were discussing something else.”

“Did it have something to do with me?”

“Some parts of it was.”

“Are you going to clue me in on it?”

“Not at this moment. Some things need to remain classified.”

“Look I understand all of that but all I want is for you to tell me what y'all said about me.”

Agent Foster stood up from the bed “You may not agree with what I am saying now, but you will when it's all said and done. Now get yourself some rest.” He said and then he walked towards the door.

"Wait, are you leaving?" I asked him, my voice sounded somewhat weary.

He stopped for a brief moment and turned his head around. "No, I'm not leaving. I'm just gonna step outside the door and talk to Agent Rome for a few minutes." He replied and then I watched him leave for the second time.

While Agent Foster busied himself outside my room door with Agent Rome, I couldn't help but think back on the near death incident that transpired between myself and that psycho bitch Bishop sent here to take my ass out. Thank God Agent Rome was here because I would've been dead.

Agent Rome acted quickly after he heard me scream for help. And once he realized what was going on, he shut her ass down. His partner, Agent George Lane, a white, taller agent with slick black hair, helped assist me and Agent Foster when it was time to escort me to another room. He also took statements from his fellow agent, Scott Rome, a few of the hospital staff as well as myself. Before I knew it, there was a room filled with black suits.

In the pecking order, Agent Foster was the HNIC in the Jersey area. I guess I was lucky. But everyone has a boss and his boss happened to be this bleached, blonde, white female, who looked like she was about five foot seven. Her name was Joyce Reed. She arrived an hour after I almost got killed. Looking at the woman, I could instantly tell that she was a tough cookie. She actually looked like she didn't take much shit from anyone. She was stern and to the point. Being that Agent Foster was a hood type of cat with a badge and she was this wonder woman type of chick, they were a force to reckon with.

Before she left my room, she and Agent Foster had a few words with one another. I overheard he tell her that he needed to have me moved to one of their safe houses with around the clock protection, led by him, but for some reason she wasn't too happy about that. And that didn't sit well with me at all. I mean, what was her problem? Did she not like me? I saw the look she gave me when she first laid eyes on me and it wasn't one of those, "I'm happy to see you"....looks either. I figured it probably had something to do with the fact that she and Agent Foster had already assigned another team of agents to protect me and now they're dead. The first one was killed inside of the apartment Bishop had me living in and the other two were killed at the service station, so shouldn't there be some kind of concern there? It seemed like every time Agent Foster was pulled away from me, Bishop found a way to slip one of his flunkies into the mix and hoped that they'd be able to create my demise. Unfortunately for them, they managed to come up short, which was why I was still alive today. I just hoped that I'd be able to keep this luck of mine up.

"We are not going to move a witness just because there was an attempt on her life." I heard that bitch tell him.

"Bullshit, Joyce," he responded. "Three months ago, the Bureau set up a witness in a five-star hotel in Atlantic City with weekly pedicures and manicures, and she was only testifying against a law firm of old ass attorneys who didn't have a bit of fight in them. Let alone come after her for testifying against them."

"You know you're exaggerating just a little bit, right?"

"I may be Joyce, but you know what we are dealing with. Bishop is one of the biggest dealers and murderers on the East Coast. He is a fucking heartless ass killer and we all know that if he took his sister out, he wont flinch if he gets another chance at Lynise. So do you really want our witness to be a sitting duck while a monster like Bishop is out there saying the hell with the FBI? Really, is that what we really want?"

Listening to Agent Foster plead my case was the best feeling in the world. I was really impressed. So, I asked myself was he really fighting for me to make sure I stayed alive or was this about some bullshit game he was playing with his boss to get his point across? I didn't know what it was. But I did know whatever drug the new nurse pumped into my veins was some good shit. The thoughts I had about the talk Joyce and Agent Foster had before she left the hospital became a distant memory. And before I knew it I had drifted off to la-la land.

When I woke up, Agent Foster was sitting in the recliner chair. I had a headache, but truthfully I was still kind of out of it. The meds I was given knocked me out for at least a couple of hours.

"How do you feel?" Agent Foster asked me.

"I feel a little groggy, but other than that I'm good.

Sean looked down at his wristwatch. "You've been out for about five hours."

"It seems like it's been longer than that." I commented. "Have any of the nurses been in here bothering me?" I wanted to know.

"You had two visits by the same nurse to do a routine check on you. The nurse made the comment that the doctor wanted to make sure you were all right especially after what you've been through. Other than that, you didn't miss anything."

"Is Agent Rome still here?" I asked, speaking slowly from the affects of the drugs I was prescribed.

"Yeah, he's sitting outside your room."

I hesitated for a moment to collect my thoughts and then I said, "Please keep him around. I swear if he wasn't around when that lady tried to kill me, I'd probably be dead right now."

Agent Foster smiled. "He's not going anywhere." He assured me.

"Good, because he knows his stuff. He took one shot and it blew a huge hole in her stupid ass!" I said as I replayed the whole event in my head. "Did y'all ever find out what her real name was?" I continued.

"Yes, we found out her name was Charlotte Livingston. And she had a wrap sheet as long as your arm. From the looks of things, she started getting in trouble back when she was ten years old."

"Damn, that's crazy! Bishop sure knows how to pick 'em." I commented.

"I think it was a bit unfortunate that Agent Rome had to kill her. Especially after finding out she had a five year old little boy."

"Oh my God! Really? She risked her life for a nigga knowing she had a little boy! That's crazy." I blurted out. I was so shocked that she'd give her life up for a nigga who didn't give a fuck about her.

"We all wondered the same thing."

So what now?" I asked. "Are you my protector for life?"

"Not for life, but for now," Agent Foster answered. "The doctor stated you need to stay another night in the hospital. After that, we are moving you to another location. Bishop is a relentless man who will stop at nothing until you're dead."

Hearing the words dead gave me a chilling feeling. But I couldn't dwell on it; I had to find out what kind of plans he had for me. "Have y'all figured out where you would be taking me?"

"I'm sorry but that's classified."

"Why is it classified? I mean it ain't like I can walk out of here and tell somebody."

"Its just protocol. And it's also for your safety." Agent Foster said flatly.

"I understand all of that. But keeping me in the dark is going to have me on edge."

"Don't work your pretty little self up. I'm gonna take very good care of you and I swear I won't let another soul get close to you."

"You promise?"

"I promise," he assured me and then he smiled.

SAFE HOUSE #1

It was the next night and out of the blue Agent Foster and his partners decided to move me. It was certainly late. As a matter of fact, it was in the wee hours of the night. Agent Foster still hadn't told me where we were going. Instead of the black SUVs I had become used to, we were traveling in a burgundy Jeep Wrangler with tinted windows. The windows weren't as dark as their standard tint but it did the job. I guess this was all about blending in. It was three of us in the car. Agent Foster sat in the backseat with me while Agent Rome sat behind the wheel.

To my understanding there were two other cars following us. One was a quarter mile behind us, and the other car was a half-mile behind them. This was FBI strategy. That whole thing of three cars traveling directly behind each other to show force was stupid. Hell, a good bomb or ambush could take out all three cars at the same time.

One of the things I was learning was that Agent Foster really was a very thorough person. He was always thinking two to three steps ahead. That wasn't me. In previous talks between us he had relayed that to me that my spontaneity and do shit now philosophy was usually what got me in trouble. He told me I needed to try thinking things out a little more. A couple of times he hurt my feelings by telling me that I was reckless. "If you had a little more common sense, you would not have gotten jammed up with Bishop and you wouldn't have been in all of this shit. Your choices in men are terrible." He said. I hated when motherfuckers tried to judge me. Stay in your lane and I'll stay in mine.

During the drive, Agent Foster had a few words for me. "We need to talk," he said to me.

Before I opened my mouth I tried to read his facial expression and when I realized that it was going to be impossible, I let out a sigh and then I said, "About what?"

"We need to talk about Bishop," he stated. "You need to know some things about his history."

"Like what?" I asked. His expression went cold. He even looked spooked. But I knew if I'd question him about the level of intimidation he had for Bishop, I'm sure he'd deny having any. Men were some funny ass creatures when it came to their masculinity. They would never let another man make them look soft under any circumstances. But before he could get into any details his phone rung. "Give me a minute, I've gotta take this call." He said and then he excused himself from the room.

It didn't take him long at all to take his call. In fact, he was back in the room in less than twenty seconds. But something was different about him. His face looked a little despondent.

"I just got a call from my supervisor Joyce saying that some local cops discovered a woman's body and it might be Agent Chrissy."

I immediately caught a lump in my throat when he told me that Chrissy's body might have been found. I knew what she had done to me was wrong, but the thought of her being dead really didn't sit well with me. I say this because, not only was Bishop killing off his enemies, he made it his business to kill off anyone close to him that knew a lot of damaging information about him. This was serious.

Instead of commenting, I held my head down and thought about all the people that suffered at the hands of Bishop. First it was Diamond and Duke Carrington and then it was Bria. In my mind, Duke and Diamond deserved to die. But Bria didn't. Never mind, she snitched on Bishop so she didn't have to serve a lot of time behind bars. Bria was a good person at heart. And I believed that if push came to shove, she and Bishop could have beat this thing together if he hadn't left her here in New Jersey while he was down in Virginia avenging Neeko's death.

"I know you're not going to want to hear this, but I'm gonna have to leave you here with Agent Rome to go to the scene where Agent Chrissy's body was found."

I looked back up. "Are you fucking serious right now?" I yelled. My heart sunk in the pit of my stomach after he had just advised me that he was leaving me once again. Was he fucking stupid? Or he just didn't give a fuck about my well-being?

"Look, I know you're worried that something may happen to you while I'm gone, but I promise you that it won't."

"That's what you said the last time." I argued. I wasn't feeling him at all with this bullshit he was talking. I was not about to be a sitting duck and allow something else to happen to me while he's away playing hero.

"Lynise, I'm sorry but I have to go. This is my investigation." He tried to explain.

I stood to my feet. "Well, if you're leaving then I'm going with you." I told him. I poked my chest out to him and held my head high. I had to show him that I was not going to back down from him.

Agent Foster shook his head. "You can't go."

"But why? I can stay in the car. I could even lay low in the back seat and no one would know that I'm even there." I reasoned.

"I'm sorry but you can't go this time." He said once again. And then he turned to leave.

I wasn't about to let him walk out on me without putting up a good fight first. I was adamant about leaving with him whether he liked it or not. "Don't walk out on me! You are not leaving me here by myself." I roared as I stormed in his tracks.

Agent Foster stopped in his tracks and turned towards me. "Lynise, you're gonna have to calm down and get a hold of yourself."

"But you lied to me! You told me that you weren't going to leave me again." I spat.

"That was before I got the phone call." He said.

Before I could challenge Agent Foster any further, Agent Rome appeared. "What's going on?"

"I just got a call from Joyce saying that a few local cops found a woman's body and that it might be Agent Chrissy." Sean explained.

"Where did they find the body?" Agent Rome's questions continued.

"In Newark's landfill."

"Wow! Someone dumped the body in a fucking garage dump landfill." Agent Rome pointed out.

"Yeah, that's what I was told." Agent Foster replied.

"Well, if that's the case then there may not be a lot of her body left with all the birds and other animals that lurk in that mountain of trash."

"I thought the same thing." Agent Foster said and then he turned his attention towards me. "Are you okay?" He asked.

"I will be after I lay down for a bit." I said and then I excused myself and headed back into the bedroom I was assigned to sleep in. Surprisingly, Agent Foster followed.

"Want me to get you something to drink?" He asked. I could tell he was concerned.

"No, I just wanna sit here for a minute." I told him.

"Well, you do that and I'm gonna run out there to see what's going on. And I promise that as soon as I'm done, I'm gonna race back over here."

As badly as I wanted to derail Agent Foster's plans to leave me behind, I didn't have enough strength to put up a fight. The thought of Chrissy's lifeless body engulfed my mind and made my heart ache. Despite the fact that she had a mission to kill me, I still felt bad for her. And to know that he threw her fucking body out in a landfill was barbaric to the tenth degree. Who kills someone and then throws their body in a pile of trash? That was the cruelest thing I had ever heard. And to know that Bishop was behind her death made me even more terrified of him. He was waging war on everyone around him and no one could see it but me.

WHAT'S NEXT?

After Agent Foster left the house I managed to get back to the bedroom I was assigned to sleep in. Agent Rome checked on me a few times before I called it a night and somehow fell asleep. But I was awakened a couple of hours later by a muffling sound and then a loud thump followed. When I opened my eyes, I couldn't see a thing because it was pitch black. I lay still for a brief minute. I even held my breath because in my mind, I wanted it to be perfectly quiet. While I tried to figure out what could've made that muffling sound, a few seconds later, I heard the sound of someone stepping on a loose wooden board. The footsteps were slow and creepy. I lifted my head up from the pillow and looked down at the foot of the bedroom door. There was a strip of light peaking in from the hallway but then all of a sudden it disappeared. The light went dark. A huge shadow engulfed the light from the hallway and it nearly sent me in a panic attack. I wanted so badly to yell out Agent Rome's name but I was afraid to open my mouth for the fear that someone other than the agents would hear me.

A moment later, someone twisted the doorknob with hopes of entering into my bedroom. But I locked it hours ago before I laid down. After the door wouldn't open, the person on the other side walked away quietly. It seemed as though they were tiptoeing. My mind raced like crazy. And I ran out of oxygen. I could no longer hold my breath so I exhaled and then I slid quietly out of bed. My heart raced rapidly. And the thought of what was going on on the other side of the door had me spooked. The fear of the unknown was weighing heavy on me. All I pictured in my mind was another one of Bishop's puppets had gotten into the safe house and I was minutes away from taking my last breath.

With little clothing on, I tiptoed over to the bedroom window and noticed there was another car parked outside. The car was black. And when I zoomed in on it, I noticed that it was a Dodge Charger. I couldn't see the plates nor could I see inside the car because the windows were tinted. This sent me in a state of panic. I immediately looked back at the bedroom door and I saw that the light from the hallway disappeared once again. So, there was no doubt in my mind that someone was standing outside the door. I couldn't take a chance allowing someone to suck the life out of me, so I turned back around towards the window, unlocked it and when I lifted it open, the security alarm went off. The blaring sounds sounded like a siren. It scared the hell out of me. And before I knew it, the bedroom door was kicked open. The light from the hallway filled the bedroom and Agent Rome appeared before my eyes with his pistol in hand pointed directly at me. "Put your hands up!" he roared. I could barely hear his voice over the alarm system, but the fact that he stood there tow-ering over me made it very clear that he didn't want me to move.

Seconds later, he stepped towards me slowly. He continued to yell words that I couldn't hear but I could see very clearly while his mouth moved. Once he got within a few feet of me, he grabbed me by my shoulders and forced me down to the floor. He buried my face into the carpet and planted one of his knees in my back. I was trying to figure out why the fuck was he handling me this way? And when I tried to communicate that to him my voice was swallowed whole by the constant blaring sounds from the alarm system.

Thankfully after being mishandled for a period of three long minutes, the alarm was finally shut down and I was lifted up and placed on the edge of the bed. Agent Rome stood in front of me and began to interrogate me. "Why were you trying to escape? Do you know you were seconds away from being shot? I had my gun cocked and ready to fire after I kicked the door in."

I was pretty shook up behind the incident that had just happened. As a matter of fact, my nerves where shattered but it didn't stop me from answering Agent' Rome's questions. "Look I was sleep but I woke up after I heard a muffling sound that sounded like somebody was being choked to death and then I heard a loud thumping noise, like someone fell down on the floor. And when I heard footsteps creeping outside my door, I got scared and tried to get the hell out of here."

Before Agent Rome could comment, the other agent joined us in the bedroom. "Is everyone all right?" he asked. He was panting like he was tired from running up the stairwell.

Agent Rome and I both turned our attention towards him. "Yes, we're fine. Ms. Carter here just explained to me why she was trying to escape." Agent Rome said.

"I was trying to save my fucking life." I spat. By this time I was getting irritated.

"She heard the same thing we heard." Agent Rome spoke up.

"Well, if you heard what I heard then why was I treated like the bad guy?" I snapped. I needed this nigga to give me a good enough explanation as to why I was slammed down to the floor. From my understanding, a federal witness wasn't supposed to be treated like this. If Agent Foster was here none of this shit would have went on. So, that brings me to believe that I'm being baby sat by fucking amateurs.

"We thought the sound was coming from upstairs which is why I came up here to check everything out. And when you opened the window to get out, I immediately thought you were the one that caused that sound we heard." Agent Rome finally explained.

"Well, it wasn't me. So, someone needs to figure out where it came from." I spat. If I could've spit fire from my mouth, I would've done it. I was utterly vexed by the way they handled things with me. And even though they thought they were doing their job, they still hadn't found out where that noise came from.

Agent Rome looked back at the other agent and ordered him to check the other two rooms of the house. Immediately after the agent walked off, I brought the car parked outside the safe house to Agent Rome's attention. "There's a Dodge Charger parked outside that wasn't there before all of this went down." I said.

Agent Rome went over to the window. "What color is it because I don't see it?" He told me.

I got up from the bed and joined him at the window and when I looked through the glass, I too did not see that Dodge Charger I saw before. I instantly became more nervous than before. "I know I'm not crazy! I just saw a black Dodge Charger parked outside of this house the same time you were walking up and down the hallway outside this room."

"Well, if you did, it's gone now."

I walked back to the bed and sat on the edge of it. I shook my head in disbelief. I knew what I saw was real and if Agent Rome didn't believe me then there was no use in dwelling on it.

While Agent Rome and I stood in the room together, the other agent yelled Agent Rome's name. "You gotta' come see this." He said.

Agent Rome ran out of the bedroom and I followed in his footsteps. We ended up in another bedroom adjacent to the right side of the house. The window had a view of the alley below and it was open. There were also a few red wires showing. Whoever did this was definitely a professional. Too bad the person wasn't able to finish his job. "Was this window opened when you came in here?" Agent Rome asked.

"Yes, it was." The agent replied and then he grabbed hold of a 20-foot Ultra-lite Urban Assault Ladder. This was some shit the Coast Guard used in rescue operations. Seeing this gave me another panic attack.

"Our location has been compromised and we gotta get her out of here," Agent Rome said.

"Now do you believe me when I told you I saw that car outside?" I asked Agent Rome.

Instead of answering my question, he grabbed me by my arm and literally escorted me out of the room and down to the first floor. After the other agent secured the room he met us on the first floor. By this time, Agent Rome had all of my things in hand and he had Agent Foster on the phone. I couldn't hear what he was saying on the other end but I could tell that he wasn't very happy after Agent Rome told him about our situation. After a few minutes of dialogue between the two, their call ended. "Agent Foster wants us to meet him at headquarters." Agent Rome told the other agent and I.

"Well, let's get the hell out of here." He said and stepped towards the front door.

"I'm gonna need you to go outside and check the perimeter before we make a move." Agent Rome instructed the other agent.

"Roger that." The agent said and then he slipped out the front door.

Agent Rome and I stood there patiently while the other agent surveyed the outside of the house. My heart did a couple of summersaults while we waited. And my mind ran every bit of fifty miles per second. All I could think about was getting out of here alive. I also thought about the possibility that Bishop could have been the one who'd tried to sneak into the safe house. And then I thought about the fact that if it was him or somebody he had employed, how in the hell had they known that I was here. Was I going to ever be safe?

PLAYING A GAME OF HIDE & SEEK

After waiting a little over two minutes the other agent radioed Agent Rome and gave him the green light to exit the house. Agent Rome walked ahead of me with his weapon drawn and ready to fire. I stood close to him the entire time. "Stay behind me." He instructed me.

"Don't worry, I will." I assured him as I looked around my surroundings as we walked down the stairs before us.

We were only a few feet away from the jeep they used to transport me, so I was counting down the steps that it would take to get us there. The other agent stood by the back door with it slightly ajar. One part of me wanted to make a run for it, but I decided against it when I saw a silver light shining on the left side of me. That light literally beamed in the left side of my peripheral vision. I was completely startled and stopped in my tracks. Agent Rome and I were standing on the last step when I froze in fear. And before I could turn in the direction where the light was coming from, Agent Rome and I both heard a loud BOOM and then we saw a firery explosion from the blast. We realized a gun had been fired and we both dove on the ground. BOOM. BOOM. BOOM. More shots rang out. I screamed my head off as I crawled behind a nearby bush. Agent Rome and the other agent returned fire. "We got another shooter on the far right side of the building across the street." Agent Rome yelled.

I laid on my stomach and covered my head with my arms. I couldn't see a thing but I heard all the commotion around me and feared the worst would happen at any moment. I kept my eyes closed and said a silent prayer. I asked God that if He'd spare my life this time around like He did the other times that I would start serving Him. I knew I said this prayer before, but for some reason I knew that I would've stayed true to my word this time around. And I almost didn't believe it, because as soon as I ended my prayer, the shooting suddenly stopped. I heard nothing from Agent Rome and the other agent so I immediately assumed that they were both dead. And knowing this, I was too terrified to move an inch or call out their names for fear that the other shooters would hear me.

I laid there in wait for a total of twenty seconds and that's when I heard the other agent call out Agent Rome's name. "Are you all right?" he asked.

"Yeah, I'm fine. Do you see any of them?"

"No, they're gone. I saw both of them run off after they ran out of ammo."

"Lynise, are you all right?" Agent Rome yelled.

I lifted my head up from behind the bush. "I'm a bit scarred up but I'll be okay." I told him.

And in a flash I was helped up onto my feet and ushered into the back of the jeep. Everyone including me was panting and trying to catch our breath. But it was truly hard. It wasn't hard for Agent Rome to jump behind the steering wheel and get us the hell out of there. I was trying to pull myself together after the shoot out. And I knew nothing in the world would help me right now but the touch of Agent Foster. I needed him now more than I ever needed him. And it was Agent Rome's job to get me to a safe place so I could see him.

It took us no time to get to the FBI's headquarters. I was placed in a room and I had to wait there for at least another hour before Agent Foster finally showed up. Of course I was angry that I had to wait in a cold ass room, but after I saw his face, being there made it all worth it. I jumped to my feet and hugged him as soon as he got within a few feet of me. I started crying and I let all my feelings out. "I don't think I can do this anymore." I cried out. "He's not going to stop until I'm dead." I continued.

Agent Foster sat me back down in the chair. And then he sat down in the chair next to me. "I know you're tired. I can see it all over your face. But, it's gonna all be over very soon. I just left from identifying Chrissy's body and if all goes well with the autopsy report and we can pen her murder on Bishop, then we're home free."

"But what if we can't?" I asked. It seemed like these investigators always get close but not close enough when it comes to getting an arrest warrant for Bishop.

"Look, don't worry. We got him right where we need him." He tried to convince me but I wasn't going for the old banana in the tail pipe. I wanted to know how was it that every time he left my side, someone always found a way to get close enough to take me out? And I asked him.

"You're always telling me not to worry. But that's not keeping me safe. Not only that, every time you leave me, someone always gets close enough to try to kill me. And that ain't sitting right with me. Someone within this department is helping Bishop and you're too fucking blind to see it."

"No, I'm aware of those possibilities. And I've got my people looking into that right now."

"Those so called people you're referring to could be the very ones who's putting us in harms way. Believe me, it's somebody close to this circle of agents you got helping you with this detail." I spat. I was fucking livid and I made sure he knew it.

He did everything within his power to calm me down. And after he did, I sat there and listened to some new information he threw my way.

"Let me tell you something about my role in this investigation." He began to say and then he hesitated. "Bishop killed my partner who also happened to be my best friend. And killing law enforcement officers is a big deal." He said and stopped once again. But I wanted to hear more of his story because it sounded like he was going somewhere with it. I just hated that he brought up the subject of best friends because I had thought about Diamond a few times and the relationship she and I had growing up together. She played a major role in my life, so to have her turn her back on me really had a major affect on me mentally. Aside from that, I still missed that bitch sometimes.

"Bishop used to be a hit man for a crime family in New York," Agent Foster began to talk again. "He actually started pretty young. Someone said he got his first kill at age fifteen. We can't prove it, but he started working for Sidney Gambino when he turned eighteen. Even as a young killer, the man was ruthless. The Italians and Sicilians hated him, but he did whatever Sidney Gambino wanted him to do. And guess what, he was the best at it."

"What? Hold on," I intervened. "So, you're telling me Bishop was connected to Old Man Gambino? The same Gambino who ran the whole east coast from New York to Florida?"

"Yeah, that's the same one."

What the fuck had I gotten myself into? Sid Gambino was a fucking whack job. There were plenty of news reports about how many people he had murdered. Unfortunately, no one would have the balls to testify so he became Mr. Untouchable to say the least.

As my mind drifted back to the day I worked at the strip club, I remembered seeing Neeko in a couple of pictures with this infamous man.

Fuck! How stupid was I? Of course Bishop worked for Old Man Gambino, Neeko and Bishop were brothers. Why didn't I make the connection before? "Oh my God! Are you telling me Bishop is a made man?"

"No, not at all," Agent Foster answered me. "Made men are 100% Sicilian and for some families, one hundred percent Sicilian or Italian, and you also have to be Catholic. No other race or religious group is accepted. And as you know, Bishop is 100% black." He continued and then he paused. Three seconds later Agent Foster picked his story back up. "Bishop was on Easy Street as long as he worked for Sid Gambino. From what you told me and the stories I heard, I think the man you met back in Virginia was signs of the old Bishop."

"Damn, what happened?" I asked out of curiosity.

"Life in the street happened," Agent Foster stated. "And now we have his ass. He is sloppy, not the man he used to be. He is prone to make mistakes and killing his sister, Bria, then Keisha—"

"Keisha?" I interrupted Agent Foster. "What you mean Keisha?" I asked in a state of panic.

Initially, Agent Foster just looked at me. He didn't say a word. But I knew that look on his face. And it wasn't an encouraging look at all. So, I knew he'd have some bad news following it. "Keisha was being moved to another safe house by some agents I knew personally, but their trip was derailed by a bunch of men wearing black masks and after they killed the agents, they shot her in the head execution style. And now we believe that the exact same men who killed her."

"He's a fucking monster." I roared.

"Yes, he is," he said and then he fell silent.

"What's wrong? Why did you stop talking?"

Agent Foster sighed heavily and then he said, "I didn't want you to know this at first, but one of the guy's left a picture of you in one of the agent's SUV and on the picture it had the words, 'you next,' meaning, he will be coming for you."

My eyes became watery. My body became numb all over again. And all I could think about was how in the world was he able to get to all of these people and kill them like that? He wasn't God! So, how much power did he really have? Someone has got to stop him before he gets to me. Or else I could kiss my life goodbye.

While I sat there with a load of fear in my heart, I looked back at Agent Foster and said, "So what's going to happen now? I know y'all have talked about which safe house you're going to take me to next."

"We're working on it right now."

"How much longer am I going to be in this shit hole? Ya'll are treating me like a criminal." I told him.

"I'm sorry they put you in here." He said and then he extended his hand. "Come on, go with me into the lounge area. You can sit in there until I get clearance to move you."

I took Agent Foster's hand and followed him to another part of the building.

A couple of hours passed before he got the green light to move me. But after his supervisor Joyce signed off on the paperwork, he escorted me to the back wing of the headquarters. This part of the building was used to processed federal prisoners in and out of the facility. "Take a seat right here and I'll be right back." He said and then he walked away.

I watched Agent Foster as he walked behind the glass partition that separated the sitting area from the office area. While I watched him sign a few pages of documents a very attractive, black woman wearing dark, blue denim jeans, a white, button down shirt, a pair of Nike Air-Max running sneakers and a FBI issued jacket with yellow letters printed on the back. She wore her hair brushed back into a ponytail. She was very young looking and her skin looked flawless. And even though her skin color was lighter than most, it was fairly noticeable that she was 100% African American. She reminded me of a younger version of Tamar Braxton. If you'd have her stand directly beside me and compared our body types, I would come out on top. There was no secret that I had a better figure than her. She was also a couple of inches taller than me too, so that gave me an edge on her as well. No man likes a tall ass woman. Men like chicks that are average in height, a small waistline and a fat ass. And knowing that I had all of those things, I was clearly the winner by more than a landslide.

Within seconds of her arrival, she was all over him. I couldn't hear their words, but it didn't take me long to see that she had a thing for Agent Foster. She couldn't stop smiling at him. In my opinion she was being a little too flirtatious to be on the clock. I sat there and watched them as they carried on with their playful ways. It was becoming unbearable. This chick was literally throwing herself all over Agent Foster and it was real evident that he was enjoying it. I even watched her as she leaned over and whispered something into his ear. She must've said something provocative because he smiled and gave her a thumb's up hand gesture. Her body language sent out a clear message to everyone around her that she'd jump at the first chance to fuck him if he'd be a willing participant. I shook my head at the thought of how far women would go for a nigga with three legs. Okay granted, I was one of those women. But, I wouldn't sweat Agent Foster the way this bitch was. What happened to having a little respect for yourself?

Ten smiles and five hand gestures later, Agent Foster grabbed the documents he signed earlier and headed back in my direction. The FBI chick followed him. I was not in the mood for what was about to go down so I braced myself. "Lynise, this is Special Agent Zachary. She will be accompanying us until we turn you over to the U.S. Marshals." He said.

She smiled as she held out her hand for me to greet her. "I know this is an unfortunate situation, but it's a pleasure to meet you anyway." She said.

Instead of extending a handshake, I gave her an unflattering expression. I had to let her know that the pleasure she'd mentioned was all hers. And why act like she was down for me? That was some fake ass shit if you'd ask me. So after she held her hand out for more than five seconds, she finally realized that I wasn't about to warm up to her and therefore she pulled her hand back. Agent Foster looked a little awkward after I embarrassed his groupie FBI friend and immediately went into damage control. "Are you feeling okay?" he asked me.

"Yeah, I'm fine." I replied sarcastically.

"Are you sure?" she chimed in, looking at me like I was fucking crazy.

I looked back at her with the look of death. I felt like she didn't have the authority to question me. I mean, just because she was an agent didn't give her right to invade in my personal space. So instead of telling her to step off, I let out a long sigh and turned my attention back towards Agent Foster. "Is it time for us to leave?" I asked him.

Agent Foster turned his focus towards Agent Zachary for a couple of seconds and then he looked back at me. "I guess it is." He finally replied.

I stood up from the bench and waited for him to lead the way. Agent Zachary walked off first. Agent Foster extended his arm and pointed in the direction that we'd be going in. "After you," he said.

I walked in the direction he pointed to. Agent Zachary walked ahead of us. You can say that she lead the way because when Agent Foster and I got to the end of the hallway, she held the door open for us.

After we exited the building, we climbed into yet another unmarked vehicle. Agent Foster climbed in the back seat with me while Agent Rome and Zachary climbed into the front seat. Agent Zachary made small talk with Agent Rome. Agent Foster chimed in a few times. For the most part, it was Agent Rome and Zachary doing the most talking. I turned my attention towards the window to collect my thoughts. I stared at the trees and high-rise buildings as we passed them. And all I could think about was all this shit I had gotten myself into. Truth be told, I was tired of going from one place to the other. So after we left the headquarters, I leaned back on the backseat and tears dropped from my eyes. This whole witness protection shit was BS anyway you looked at it. And if someone doesn't get Bishop before he gets to me, then what good am I going to be to anybody?

With Keisha, Bria and Diamond dead, I was the only person left to bring Bishop's grimy ass down. So, I knew he'd move hell and high water to get to me. In the end, will I survive him?

Too bad I didn't have the answer to my own question. And I didn't have a plan as to how I planned to stay alive. All I had was a hunch that if things didn't go in my favor, I was going to be one dead bitch.

The next safe house was definitely a hideaway spot. I had no idea New Jersey had areas where real estate properties built land that's no congested. This was something new for me. The safe house they set me up in was off the grid in a big way. There wasn't another house in the area for at least one mile. This land would be a drug dealer's dream.

Once we were inside the house all the agents teamed up to inspect the entire home and when they cleared all the areas, they gave me the green light to move about freely. I was instructed by Agent Foster not to leave the house under no circumstance. And then he instructed me to stay away from the windows as well, which I had no problems with. But when Agent Zachary opened her mouth and instructed me to let her know when I needed to use the bathroom, I took that thing to heart. I mean who the fuck was she? I was a grown ass woman. And the last time I remembered telling my mother when I had to use the fucking bathroom, was when I was five years old. So, what was her problem? "Why do I have to tell you when I gotta go to the bathroom? I didn't have to do that when I was at the last place." I questioned her.

Before Agent Zachary could utter one word, Agent Foster came to her rescue. He knew I was about to blast her ass so he did everything in his power to diffuse the situation. "It was my idea." He interjected. "We just want to take extra precautionary measures to prevent from having another incident that happened at the last place."

"Yeah, okay." I commented and then I rolled my eyes. I walked away from both of those clowns. I knew deep inside my heart that that idea hadn't come from Agent Foster because if it had, he would've implemented it from day one.

I left both of them standing in the living room area of the safe house and excused myself to the bedroom they assigned to me. I figured I had had enough of Agent Zachary for one day.

SOMEONE PLEASE WAKE ME UP

"What's up, bitch, how you doing?" Diamond asked me. She popped up out of nowhere as I walked into the unfamiliar restaurant. She wore all black so I assumed she was the hostess. We were once the best of friends, now she was dead. Because of her heavy involvement with Duke Carrington, Bishop and his henchmen murdered her. Unfortunately, she picked the wrong bad guy to follow. More importantly, she fucked with the wrong bitch—me.

I looked at her from head to toe. Her face was very ashy. And her body was engulfed in smoke. "Please excuse my appearance," she said. "Once you been in hell for a little while, you will get used to it."

I didn't respond because I realized I was having a dream . . . actually it was a bad nightmare.

"Where am I?" I asked her as I continued to look around at my surroundings.

She shook her head. "You still don't get it, do you?" was her response. "Girl, you are where you belong. Where all of the do-or-die chicks, hustlers, players and so-called gangstas belong."

I didn't say anything. This stupid ass bitch and I didn't belong in the same room, let alone the same location. So how we ended up in the same restaurant and at the same table, puzzled the hell out of me.

"Don't act so surprised," Diamond continued. "Yes, you are in hell and since I was the closest to you, the King of Hades sent me down to greet you. To welcome you to Hell."

I still didn't say anything. Diamond, Satan and anyone else were sadly mistaken if they thought I belonged down here. "This is not Hell," I said.

Diamond didn't say anything but then she suddenly opened her blood red and black shirt and what I saw scared the living shit out of me. I didn't see her breasts or a bra or even her empty skin. I was watching a flaming inferno burn inside of Diamond's body. I even saw the souls of others trying to escape the inferno, but there was no escape.

For whatever reason, I didn't move. I just stared in disbelief. Was this what I was meant to do—living in hell for the rest of my days. I couldn't believe this shit. This was not my destiny. I had a whole life to live. I still had babies to make, a husband to drive me crazy and plenty of dick to be fucked and sucked. This was bullshit! This was someone else's destiny, not mine.

"Finally getting to see me after you had Bishop and his crew murder me is really fucking your head up, huh?" Diamond interrupted my thoughts. She was grimacing the entire time she spoke. I could see through her firey eyes how she'd swallow me whole if she could. The writing was on the wall clear as day. "What's wrong? You're scared to talk shit to me now that you're all alone."

"I'm not afraid of you Diamond and I'm not afraid of this place. You got what you deserved. Point blank." I challenged her. "I loved you like a sister and you betrayed me for a nigga who didn't a fuck about either of us."

"I didn't betray you. He wanted me and you know it. He wanted me from the beginning" Diamond belted out. Her eyes turned redder than ever before.

"I'm not gonna stand here and listen to his mess. You're crazy!" I said and then I turned my back on her.

"Don't turn your back on me!" she roared. And then a force of wind whirled me back around. I was standing in the exact spot I was before.

"What do you want with me?" I yelled at her. I was tired of being in this God forsaken place. I wanted to get away from her.

"I want you to take a long look at me because this is how you will be when your day comes."

"I'm not coming here so you can forget that." I told her. I was very adamant about what I had just said. Diamond was going to be in this fucking hellhole by herself. I can count on my fingers and toes all the times she fucked people over. From getting niggas robbed to fucking other chick's men, Diamond had created a whirlwind of karma and now she's finally reaping all the bullshit she sowed into other people's lives.

Diamond continued to taunt me about how and when I would be joining her in this hot pit until I had enough and made myself wake up. I woke up in a cold sweat and I was so happy to see the light of day. But I couldn't get my mind off the conversation Diamond and I had in my dream. The fact that she thought Duke loved her was a fucking joke to me. And what really put the icing on the cake for me was how she believed that it was my fault that Bishop murdered her. Granted Bishop was a fucking monster, but she caused all of that shit that happened back in Virginia. Case closed.

I wiped the sweat from forehead and neck area. And then I laid there in bed trying to make sense of that dream. Mulling over the idea that the dream I just had could have had meaning behind it, I stopped to think about the possibility that I could end up in hell. My life hadn't always been a box of cherries and I'd also had my fair share of fucking up nigga's lives too. The only upside to the whole idea was that I was still a good person at heart, so would that make up for the bad shit I did?

On another note, my once knight and shining armor—Bishop would get a one-way ticket to hell with no problems. With all the bodies he had, he'd be welcomed with open arms. The way I was told how he had niggas to roll up on Keisha and those three agents and just killed the fuck out of all of them was simply barbaric. And to accomplish that mission in broad daylight was some psycho type of shit. No one would expect to see something go down like that unless it was on TV.

Now I know Agent Foster or Rome didn't want to show any emotions or feelings, but I knew they had to be a little bit afraid of Bishop. This nigga was definitely a grim reaper. And they knew it too.

The thought of him being in Neeko's strip club when it blew up and then walked away from it unharmed made me wonder if this motherfucker really was a ghost. Then to murder Duke and his boys up the way he did, just added to the legend of the man called Bishop. He seemed to be invincible. Especially since he hasn't been caught after all the terror he has inflicted on people. I just hoped and prayed that Agent Foster and his A-Team knew what they were dealing with and handled things accordingly.

After having a ton of thoughts about Bishop's reign, I got up from the California-style bed in the master bedroom on the top floor of the new safe house. The bedroom itself was the size of the apartment I shared with Diamond in Virginia. I just needed to go to the little girl's room. So, when my feet hit the floor, Agent Foster, who was sleeping on a sofa on the other side of the bedroom, suddenly rose and his gun was pointed at me. He literally scared me too death.

"Agent Foster, it's me," I said as I raised my arms high in the air.

"I'm sorry," he said as he wiped sleep from his eyes. "I'm sorry, Lynise, I didn't know it was you standing there."

"I can see that," I replied sarcastically. Truthfully speaking, I need to encourage his ass to get a set of fucking bifocals. I would've been fucked up if he 'd pulled his trigger. So, I thank God he didn't.

It didn't take me long at all to use the bathroom. And after I was done I headed back into the bedroom. But instead of seeing Agent Foster on the sofa, he was up and looking out the window.

"Is somebody out there?" I asked very nervously.

"No, I was just checking out the area around us," he said. "I assure you Lynise, we are good here. No one knows about this place and as you noticed when we came in, if Bishop is able to penetrate this place, then we all deserve to die."

Maybe he was right. We were inside a compound outside of Patterson, New Jersey. The house was a three-level condo and by far the nicest house I had ever been in. Sean was right. He had at least eight agents that I knew of throughout the house and outside. There were agents on every level, plus outside.

I figured that if everyone in this house held his own, then we'd all be good until Bishop was picked up. I was the only one alive out of Bria, Keisha and Chrissy to testify against Bishop. I was the only one left out of Diamond, Duke, Neeko and his baby mama Katrina. I guess I was more of a ghost than Bishop. So, that should say a lot about my resilience. I never realized how badly my life had turned out until after Agent Foster first introduced himself to me and told me about the investigation surrounding Bishop's drug enterprise and Bria's disappearance. That day was undeniably one of the worse days of my life. Bishop's psychopath ass definitely knew how to throw a party in my honor.

I joined Agent Foster at the window. I peered over his shoulders to get a view of what he was looking at. "Look, I don't know how much longer I'm going to be able to take this witness protection bullshit. I mean, aren't I supposed to feel safe?"

"Yes, of course you do.

"Well, I don't. And I haven't felt safe since Bishop had someone drive that fucking car into my living room."

"It's normal to feel the way you're feeling. But it'll all go away sooner than you think." He said and then he turned his focus back outside.

BE AFRAID, BE VERY AFRAID

Boredom and fear makes for a bad marriage. It's a relationship that's not compatible for me. Maybe that's why I was stir-crazy. To put it mildly, this place was getting the best of me and I couldn't handle it any longer. It had been four days and I was forbidden to leave this house so I was about to pull my fucking hair out. I couldn't even step outside to get a breath of fresh air. The only thing that kept me sane was the fact that Agent Foster was here with me, but for the most part he was always in work mode. So, you can't win them all.

From time to time I'd get a little horny and I'd dream of the moment that Agent Foster would let me release some of the steam I've got built up inside of me. I made reference a few times to him that I needed to get fucked. In my mind it was the only thing that would calm me down. Aside from the boredom, a sense of fear was beginning to attack my patience. I had to admit that Bishop was inside of my head and he was fucking me in the worse of ways. I wasn't sleeping well. Tossing and turning throughout the night was nothing compared to every time I woke up, Agent Foster, the man of the night, was also awake and having problems sleeping. I think somewhere in the back of my mind I was hoping he'd come on to me and show me what he was working with. Too bad it didn't happen. Quiet as kept, Agent Foster appeared to be more worried than I was. I knew he'd never admit it, but at the end of the day the writing was definitely on the wall.

It was a Tuesday afternoon and I was hungry. I was actually on the first floor sitting on a huge sofa in the family room watching TV. That morning I had been in another room on the second floor. This particular room had no windows at all. It didn't even have one of those one-way mirrors to look into the room next to it. It was an interview room and while I sat next to Agent Foster, a few minutes later the Assistant US Attorney was led in the room.

Agent Foster was kind of leery about this safe house visit, due to the past security breaches that involved me. Not to mention, the breach that also caused Keisha's death sentence. But unfortunately, Agent Foster had no other choice in the matter. It was either I go to the US Attorney's headquarters or he'd have to come to me.

The objective for today's meeting was solely for the purposes of debriefing me. The short, pudgy guy was supposed to be the best in the attorney general's office but I begged to differ. Immediately after we were formally introduced, he read off a list of potential charges against Bishop. He had a video recording of the shooting in Atlantic City and even though Bishop wore a ski mask, I was still able to identify him. I had to admit that after watching the footage for only a few minutes gave me a damn headache and worse, it made me more and more afraid of his wrath. He had a gun in each hand and the way he handled those weapons was like a work of art. I always heard that trying to fire two guns at the same time was hard as shit. In the real world, being able to shoot straight with two pistols took practice, patience and a certain amount of courage and strength. Unfortunately for everyone in this room, Bishop had all four of those things. To put it mildly, I had become terrified.

I gave the assistant US Attorney all the information I knew about Bishop and the drugs he was involved in. I even gave him bits and pieces of information about our time together in Virginia. I couldn't tell him everything because I would have incriminated myself, so I stayed away from the topic concerning the murders he committed. After everything was said and done he asked if I needed an attorney and I told him that it wouldn't be necessary. I trusted and believed in Agent Foster and every documented affidavit I signed was told to me by Agent Foster that it was my get out of jail free card. The recordings from the wiretaps I supplied to them before the first two agents were killed were also apart of the deal. So, from where I stood, I would be in the clear after everything was said and done.

Once the US Attorney had everything he needed he picked up his things and left. A few minutes later I made the comment about how hungry I was. Luckily Agent Foster had already thought ahead and had Agent Zachary to go and fetch everyone in the house some food. When she returned, Agent Foster yelled for me to come into the eating area. I met him a couple of minutes later and took a seat at the table.

"Here you go," he said as he brought me a container of food. He handed me a Styrofoam carryout container from a nearby Soul Food restaurant containing baked chicken, broccoli, potato and cheese casserole, corn on the cob and cornbread. I was eating like a queen and trying my best to remain lady-like.

Agent Foster, Rome and Zachary did a little small talk while they ate. I sat there in silence while Agent Zachary entertained both men. She made it very obvious that she loved the attention they gave her. I sucked my teeth and sighed heavily a couple of times to let her know I was tired of hearing her fucking voice. Every word she uttered from her lips made me cringe. "Are you okay?" she blurted out.

I looked up from my container of food and gave her the nastiest look I could muster up. "No. As a matter of fact, I'm not." I replied sarcastically.

"What's the problem?" her questions continued.

Agent Rome and Foster stopped eating and waited for me to answer Agent Zachary's question. "You're the problem." I didn't hesitate to say. "You've been the problem since you walked on the scene."

"How is it that I'm the problem when I'm being paid to protect you?" she asked me.

"Ahhh please, cut it out. You didn't come here to protect me!" I roared. I wanted to expose her for the slut she was.

Agent Rome sat there in silence. But Agent Foster once again came to the bitch's rescue. "All right Lynise, that's enough. She's our colleague. And she's one of the best Special Agents this bureau has."

"No disrespect Agent Foster, but I don't give a damn what you say she is. In my eyes, she's a fucking undercover whore. And everybody in this house knows it. I mean come on, we know she agreed to come on this detail because she wants to fuck you." I spat. I really wanted to spit fire at Agent Foster's ass since he kept running to her aid. Agent Zachary was a big girl, so he needed to let her fight her own battles.

Instead of retaliating and lashing me with her tongue, she burst into laughter. Agent Zachary chuckled. This whore laughed at me like I was a fucking clown. Was I walking around with a red nose and white paint on my face and didn't know it? I mean what was her deal?

"You're funny. You know that?" she commented.

"And what's your point?" I questioned her. I wanted her to say something foul so I could curse her ass out. Her presence here gave me a really bad taste in my mouth. She wanted everything to be about her. She pranced around this safe house like the world revolved around her ass. But in reality, it wasn't. And I was the perfect person to rain on her parade.

"Okay Lynise, I said that's enough." Agent Foster spoke up once again. His tone was sterner than the last time so I knew he was serious.

I started to challenge Agent Foster but I decided against it. I figured why try to get my point across to him when I knew he'd side with Agent Zachary in the end?

A few minutes later, I closed my container of food and got up from the table. "I'm gonna finish eating in my room." I told Agent Foster and then I exited the kitchen.

I had no idea Agent Foster would come behind me. I was shocked when he appeared at the entryway of the bedroom only seconds after I had entered into the room myself. I was sitting on the edge of the bed with my container of food opened when he got my attention.

"I want to apologize to you for the way things went down a few minutes ago." he said as he stood before me.

"Don't worry about it. I'm cool. You said your peace and I said mine." I said hoping he'd take the hint that I didn't want to be bothered.

Surprisingly, he didn't take the hint. Instead, he took a seat on the bed next to me. "Look Lynise," my main reason for coming in here was to reassure you that every agent in this house came together for one reason and that reason was to make sure that we kept you safe. Now I don't know where all of that attitude you got came from, but you need to take it back where you got it from. Getting on Agent Zachary's bad side isn't a smart move on your part. She's a very great agent and she'll risk her life for you. So, would you please show her a little more appreciation?"

"Okay, she may be a great agent, but why do I have to show her gratitude? I mean, isn't that her job?"

"Yes it is. But Lynise, this back and forth stuff between you and Agent Zachary has got to stop. We're already dealing with shit coming in from the outside. So, we gotta' counteract that negative shit by making the atmosphere in here as serene as possible."

I understood where Agent Foster was coming from. And I had to admit that he was right. But, I couldn't get the thought out of my head that I had to co-exist with his colleague while we were under the same roof. I didn't ask her to come help babysit me. So at the end of the day, I figured he needed to go and step to her because she came into my space. "Okay, check this out, I'll chill out on my end if you promise to keep her away from me." I said.

"How do you propose I do that?" he asked. He seemed a bit puzzled.

"Just tell her not to talk to me. If she has any questions for me, tell her to direct them to you." I explained.

Agent Foster cracked a smiled. "You're kidding right?"

"No, I'm dead serious." I replied.

Agent Foster thought for a moment and then he let out a long sigh. "Okay, I'll tell you what, as long as you keep the drama to a minimum, I'll keep Agent Zachary from communicating with you."

"You promise?" I gave him a serious look.

"You've got my word. But, you gotta promise me that you're gonna keep your end of the bargain."

"Deal." I said. And then a few seconds later I was able to smile. It felt like a weight was lifted from my shoulders. So, I felt relieved.

LATER THAT NIGHT

So far Agent Foster kept his word by keeping Agent Zachary away from me. I hadn't heard a peep out of her since the incident that happened earlier in the kitchen. For the most part I'd been hanging out in my room. I had a television with digital cable on it so I was cool. And in the middle of watching an episode of "Love and Hip Hop", I had to use the bathroom so I got up and left my room.

I had to walk by the bedroom where Agent Foster slept, so when I passed it and saw him sitting in a chair staring out of the window I stopped to ask him if he was all right.

"I'm good," he replied. "I'm just sitting here looking at all the land surrounding this house."

"Yeah, we're definitely out in the boonies"

Agent Foster let out a long sigh. "Yeah, and it's kinda making me wish I was home relaxing in my own bed." He stopped talking and looked straight ahead like he was in a trance. I waited for him to say something else, but his mouth wouldn't move.

"Can I ask you a question?" I spoke up.

"Yeah, sure. What's on your mind?"

"I noticed that your mood changed after you got back from I.D'ing Agent Chrissy's body. So I just wanted to know if it effected you?"

Agent Foster turned around in the chair to face me. "Yes, of course seeing her like that effected me. If you knew her as long as I did, you would understand what I am about to tell you. See, when I think back on how hard she worked before that incident happened it disappointed me because she had a promising career with the bureau. And then when I think about how she allowed that bum to manipulate her into throwing her life away I become enraged because now she's dead."

I sat there and listened to Agent Sean pour out his feelings about Agent Chrissy's demise. He was definitely broken up about it and the fact that he didn't hide it made me look at him from a different light.

After he spilt his guts about his feelings for Agent Chrissy he went into the spiel about how he first met her. "You won't believe it but I met Agent Morales over five years ago on a business trip to Hartford, Connecticut. She heard me speak at a conference and afterwards she introduced herself. She told me she spoke six languages and that she wanted so badly to work for the bureau. So, I pulled a few strings to speed up the process and then it went on from there. After she got her security clearance, she was in."

"Oh, so now I see the feelings of betrayal. Especially with her killing Agent Morris and Paz." I told him.

"Exactly," he said in a low voice. "A few of the department heads are trying to figure out how she met and started working for Bishop as we speak. I just wished that I was around to stop it before it all went down. This was my investigation. Pax and Morris were only filling in and now they're both gone. You can't imagine how I felt when I had to break the news to their families." He explained.

Watching Agent Foster as he wore his heart on his shoulders made me feel like I was back in Neeko's club behind the bar, listening to motherfuckers' problems and occasionally giving them advice. The only difference with this conversation was that I was talking to an FBI Agent and what we were discussing involved keeping my ass alive. Talk about life's issues.

Twenty minutes into our conversation, I began to lose interest in the subject surrounding Chrissy. Granted it was sad that she got killed, but when I think about the fact that she tried to end my life, my feelings towards her started to change. At the end of the day, she wasn't a victim, I was. Besides that, she sold out her counterparts for a street nigga who probably only promised her his hard dick and a pack of bubblegum. Okay Bishop was a handsome and powerful cat, but if I were in her position, I would not have jeopardized my job and my freedom just to kill a bitch from the south. No way! Bishop would've had to pay me a ton of money before I'd agree to pull the trigger like she did.

I briefly looked into the hallway and then I looked back at Agent Foster. "I can't believe your little girlfriend hasn't come in here to check on you." I waited for his reaction but surprisingly he didn't take the bait. However, he patted my legs twice and then he changed the subject.

"I just got a call from Joyce and we might be getting you out of here sooner than we thought." He said.

My heart jumped for joy. The thought of being able to go about freely and not being caged inside of a safe house made me beam with happiness. But all of those feelings I had came crashing down around me when Agent Foster opened his mouth and said, "If all goes according to plan, you'll be in the Marshals' custody within the next four to five days and then they'll take you off to one of their secured locations and you'll be safe and sound."

"What about you? Where will you be?" I wanted to know. My entire mood changed at that very moment.

"I'm gonna be hanging out at the office trying to get everything ready for your case."

"So, you're not gonna be with me?"

"I can't. Once you're in their hands, that's it. My job will be done."

"Well, I've already told you before that I'm not going with them unless you're going too. With everything that happened, I won't allow myself to trust anyone else."

"I completely understand your concerns. And they are very valid. But this arrangement is out of my hands."

"Well, there's gonna be some upset folks because if I can't have my way, then there's a lot of shit that isn't going to get done." I expressed.

Agent Foster saw the disappointment in my eyes. But seeing it and doing something about it were two different issues. I just hoped he'd take heed and make this situation right.

After he and I talked about a few more issues, I said good night and walked off towards the bathroom. It was long over due.

On my way back to my room, I looked back into the room where Agent Foster was, but he was gone. I figured he left to go and see where Agent Zachary was. I mean, I did bring her name up, so curiosity must've gotten the best of him.

Back in my room, I laid on the bed and pictured Agent Foster smiling at me while crawling on top of me. I could see him fucking my brains out as we speak. Not only was he cute, his smile was radiant. If there was one flaw on him, I hadn't seen it. And if I had to give him a number one through ten based on his looks, then I'd give him a ten because this guy was handsome. He looked like he had a big dick too. So, tell me who wouldn't want him to fuck their brains out? He was eye candy to the tenth power. And he knew how to protect me, which was initially why I had become attracted to him.

I just wished that I could get him to run off with me. We'd make a good team. With his expertise in law-enforcement and my street creditability, he and I could conquer the world. I know Agent Zachary would die if she found out Agent Foster and I ran off with each other. This bitch would probably jump off a bridge and kill herself. And I swear, I'd love to see the day when it happened. Maybe then she'd get the message that I'm the HBIC around here. But then again, maybe she won't.

THE DEVIL HAS A FACE

Besides the normal everyday drama, yesterday ended pretty good day. It was nice just having a conversation with Agent Foster without Agent Zachary lingering around. After our little chat ended, I dozed off to sleep. And I slept well too. It was probably the best sleep I had had since we had been at the compound. It was a commodity and I was enjoying it. That's why I was pissed when the phone woke me up. It wasn't my phone. I didn't have a phone. It was Agent Foster's phone. I was surprised to see him asleep on the loveseat only a few feet away from my bed. Normally he'd sleep in the other bedroom or in the living room area, but I guessed he had something else on his mind last night.

His cell phone rang at least five times and he didn't answer. Instead of going to voicemail, the caller called back immediately.

After Agent Foster said hello in a groggy and sleepy voice, he suddenly sat completely up. The moon was full and it was shining through the bedroom window. I turned on the light from the lamp that sat on the nightstand. Sean had a serious look on his face. The caller was talking.

Then Agent Foster said, "You can't make no demands over here. I'm running this show!" he snapped and then he fell silent.

I suspected the caller was doing the talking during this time because Agent Foster's face gave off some excruciating expressions as if he was in pain of some sort. I sat there alert and I was very anxious to find out what was going on. But I knew there was no way he would involve me at this point. So, I sat there and waited until he was done with his phone conversation.

"Why don't you just give yourself up?" Agent Foster asked the caller. And that's when I knew he was speaking with Bishop.

Immediately after my suspicion was confirmed, my heart started beating erratically. I got up from the bed and rushed towards the bedroom window. I peeped around the mini blinds to see if I could see anything beyond the house. But, it was too dark to see anything. So, I turned my focus back on Agent Foster, who by this time had rushed out of the bedroom. I knew he was going to one of the other agents so I raced behind him.

I followed Agent Foster to the other side of the house where Agent Zachary and Agent Rome where posted up. They were up talking to one another in the living room. The television had been turned off, so when they heard Agent Foster burling towards them, he immediately got their attention. No one said a word. When I entered the room, all eyes were on Agent Foster. He took center floor. "If you don't hand over what belongs to me, then I'm gonna kill everyone in your family staring with your mother." I heard Bishop say. By this time Agent Foster had him on speakerphone. Everyone in the room could hear the entire conversation.

"Touch my family and I will hunt you down and kill you slowly." Agent Foster threatened.

Bishop burst into laughter. He must've found Agent Foster's words to be humorous. "You're a fucking joke!" he began to say. "You wouldn't be able to find me even if I gave you a GPS. You and your agent buddies are amateurs so face it. I'm untouchable. Now, do everyone a favor and hand Lynise over to me."

Hearing my name sent me into a panic attack. My head started spinning in circles and I couldn't stop it. I stood there in shear fear. Bishop just said that he wanted Agent Foster to hand me over to him. Now what kind of shit was that? And how in the hell did he get his number? Was I missing something here?

"Come get her." Agent Foster snapped. There was no denying that Bishop and his demands enraged Agent Foster and he made it known.

"Don't worry, I will." Bishop said in a cold and calculated manner. And then a couple seconds later, the phone went silent.

Agent Foster said hello and then he pulled the phone away from his ears and immediately noticed that Bishop had disconnected their call. "Is he gone?" Agent Rome asked.

Agent Foster said, "Yes, he's gone." And then he looked at me.

Following his lead, Agent Rome and Agent Zachary turned their attention on me as well. I stood there with a whole bunch of emotions dangling inside of me. I didn't know whether I wanted to run and hide or run into Agent Foster's arms.

"Are you okay?" he asked me.

I didn't know what to say or how to answer him? I mean, was that a trick question? How was I supposed to feel? I had just heard one of the most hated men on earth tell a federal agent that he was coming to get me. The horror in Bishop's voice spooked me. It literally gave me chills and I wanted to run for cover. But I stood still. I couldn't move my feet. It was like I was paralyzed or something.

Thankfully Agent Foster stepped towards me because I wasn't about to help myself. "Come over here and take a seat." He instructed me as he led me to the love seat across from Agent Rome and Agent Zachary.

I took a seat on the chair and tried to regroup. I tried to get my mind to focus. But I couldn't. I really needed someone to help me so I placed my hand over my forehead and said, "Oh my God, he's on his way over here. What are we going to do?" I panicked.

Agent Foster placed his hand on my right shoulder. "He's not gonna find us. So, don't worry."

I placed my face in the palm of my hands. I couldn't stand the sight of everyone around me. Nor could I stand looking at the interior of this room. I wanted to block everything out so I closed my eyes once my entire face was covered. I said a silent prayer and begged God to help me.

THE HUNT WAS ON

Agent Foster stood over top of me for the next few minutes trying to calm me down but it seemed like nothing he did worked. Agent Rome even tried to make me feel a little more at ease but I couldn't get Bishop's words out of my head. While I racked my brain trying to figure out what I was going to do, Agent Foster instructed Agent Rome to watch me while he stepped out of the room. He held his cell phone in his hand as he walked away. Before he stepped around the corner, I saw him put the phone up to his ear. I heard him pacing back and forth in the hallway. A few seconds later I heard him say, "Cee Cee, I need you to take mom to your house for a couple of days. And don't let her go back home until I call you back and give you the word. And if she asks you why she has to leave her house, just tell her I will explain it to her later." Then he fell silent. Normally I'd hear the other person talking through the receiver, but this time it was impossible because he was too far away.

"Well, if you have any problems, just call me back and let me know." He said and then he fell silent once again. And when he turned the corner to enter back into the living room area, that's when I realized that he had ended his call.

"I take it, you believed what he said when he told you he was going to kill your family." I spoke up.

"You can never be too careful in my line of work." He replied.

"So, what makes you think he won't find out where we are and hunt us down?" I asked him. And he needed to give me a damn good answer. Whether he believed it or not my situation wasn't any different from his mothers. Bishop was known for carrying out his threats, so if it meant that he'd kill who ever to get to me, everyone needed to wake up and take heed. Bishop was an American terrorist and they'd better recognize it.

While I continued to make it a big issue for us to leave the safe house, Agent Rome pulled Agent Foster to the side. A few minutes later, Agent Foster stepped away from Agent Rome and walked back into the hallway. Once again, I heard him speaking to someone on the phone. And when he made reference that we needed clearance to leave, I knew he was talking to his supervisor Joyce.

One part of me wanted to jump for joy knowing that he was making an effort to get me out of here, but then again, I knew he was talking to Joyce. And for some reason or another, I didn't think Joyce liked me. From day one, it seemed like she didn't favor anything that concerned me. Who knew what she would say this time.

"Let's pack up your things and get out of here." Agent Foster said to me as soon as he entered back into the living room.

I let out a sigh of relief. I couldn't believe what I was hearing. "Are you serious? She said we could leave?" I asked him.

"Yes, now let's get a move on it," he instructed me.

I got up from the love seat and rushed back to my room. I grabbed everything on sight and threw it in my carry-on bag. I also made sure I grabbed my purse that had the money and the dope I had stolen from Bishop the day he had someone crash a car into the apartment he and I sometimes shared.

While I was preparing to leave I heard Agent Foster running around the safe house. I also heard him yelling out orders to the other agents. Some time after that, he showed up to the room where I was. And when he approached the entryway of the door he made his presence known. "How long will it take you to put on your clothes?" he asked me.

"If you close the door I can have it done in less than a minute." I said.

"Well, let's do it. Chop! Chop!" he said and then he closed the bedroom door.

"I know. I know." I yelled through the door.

Finally after getting my clothes and myself together, I made it back to the living room in less than three minutes flat. And from there I was escorted outside with the other agents in tow.

I was now standing close to Agent Foster. He looked at me, but didn't say a word. Before I knew it, we were in cars and moving our asses to safety. Agent Foster hadn't said it out of his mouth, but I knew he felt deep in his heart that Bishop would find us. Bishop was a very resourceful man and what Bishop wanted, he got; even if it meant taking someone's life for it.

Agent Foster, Agent Rome and I were all in the same vehicle while Agent Zachary and the other agents crawled into the other vehicles. And then the strangest thing happened. There were a total of three vehicles and we all went in different directions. What the fuck was going on? I didn't say anything until we stopped and met another SUV, a Nissan Pathfinder. It was white with dark tinted windows. I assumed the guy who got out of the SUV was an agent because the windbreaker he had on had FBI embroidered on it in big gold letters.

Agent Foster and Rome jumped out of the truck and I was instructed to follow suit. Agent Rome still had my travel bag and my purse in hand. And surprisingly enough, after we got into the Pathfinder, the other agent got in the SUV we were in and there were only a few words passed between Agent Foster and the other agent. Agent Foster and Rome put their phones in a bag and gave it to the agent. The agent, in turn, gave Agent Foster and Rome a bag. I would learn later that the bag contained new cell phones. I was absolutely tripping out over all of this shit that was going on?

"Can somebody tell me where the hell are we going?" I asked sarcastically. I was getting pretty tired of all the nonverbal communication everybody was doing. It was time for someone to open up their damn mouths.

"We're going to Virginia," Foster stated.

"What? Are you serious?" I asked.

"Very serious," Agent Foster answered. "I think it's better this way."

"Please tell me you're joking." I continued talking sarcastically.

"Me and Agent Rome feel that Virginia would be the last place anyone would suspect for you to be. We'll only be there for a few days and once the U.S. Attorney wraps up this case, we'll be back here to finish what we started and then it'll all be over. You can go your way and we can go ours."

"So, you think it's that simple?" I snapped. "Do you know who the fuck we're dealing with? Bishop is a fucking psycho and y'all are taking this thing lightly."

"Lynise, will you just please calm down and trust me? I can assure you that we have this thing under control." Agent Foster tried to assure me. But I wasn't hearing him at all.

"The last time you told me y'all had things under control, I almost got my fucking head blown off. Y'all are the worst set of FBI agents I've ever seen. And it seems like every time I turn around someone in your department is working for Bishop. There are leaks all over the fucking bureau. So, how can I trust y'all? I mean are you listening to yourself? Or am I just fucking crazy?" I yelled. I was fucking livid with this whole operation. If I were ever able to get the first chance to sneak away from these stupid ass niggas with badges, I would run away and they'd never find me.

"No one knew about the house we were staying at. The house actually belongs to the friend of the deputy director. After the incident at the hospital and the last safe house, I decided that that spot would be great for us."

"So, if it was all that great and no one knew about it, why did you move me?" I questioned him because the shit he was saying wasn't adding up to me.

"I moved you so you could feel safe. It's our job to stay a couple steps ahead of the enemy. And that's what we intend to do." he continued to explain the situation to me. It seemed like every word he uttered went through one ear and directly out the other side.

"Do I have any say in where y'all are taking me?" I wondered aloud.

"No. I'm sorry you don't." he said to me. "But to put you a little more at ease, we have several secured safe houses so you will be in good hands."

"You said that the last time," I said.

"Yes, I did. But we've got things intact now."

"Well, since we're going to Virginia, can you tell me what city we'll be staying in?" I asked. My heart started pounding fast.

"We're gonna be staying in Newport News." Agent Foster said calmly.

"Are you fucking crazy? What are you trying to do? Take me to an early grave?" I asked. Newport News was to damn close to Virginia Beach. The thought of it made me sick to my stomach.

"Of course not. I can promise you that there will be no mishaps of any kind once we touch down at that location." He tried to explain.

I instantly had a headache. Primarily because I knew Agent Foster was blowing smoke up my ass and the fact that two brothers who were known by the initials TC and AC were waiting on me back in Virginia. Those two men were also on the list of niggas who wanted me dead because of Duke Carrington's untimely death. I say take that shit up with Bishop. Bishop was the one who pulled the fucking trigger. So, was I jumping into another pile of shit? And am I having another string of bad luck? I will say this though, if I didn't have bad luck, I wouldn't have any luck at all.

HIGHWAY 95

I was cramped up in the back of this damn SUV we had to travel down to Virginia in. During the six-hour drive, Agent Foster only allowed the truck to stop one time. "This will be the only time we stop until we reach Virginia so if you gotta' use the potty, I suggest you do so now." He advised me.

After I took care of my female duties I hopped back into the truck and held my bladder until our final stop, which was Newport News. Agent Foster stopped the truck in front of this spot that looked like a halfway house. The building was a two-story triplex with iron bars covering the windows. Nothing about it was appealing at all. "This is home sweet home." Agent Foster blurted out.

"How long do we gotta stay here?" I asked as soon as I stepped out of the truck. We were about ten minutes in driving distance from Patrick Henry Mall, which was a beautiful mall, but it seemed like we were way across town in a low-income urban community. This place really sucked and I made it known.

"If all goes well, we won't have to be here longer than a week."

"I hope it's soon because this place creeps me out. I mean, I'm grateful and all to be alive but my living arrangements gotta' get better than this. I'm used to staying in luxury condos and five-start hotels. So, I am truly out of my element."

Agent Rome got out of the truck after I did and said, "You'll be just fine. No one is going to bite you."

Agent Foster grabbed me by my arm and began to escort me towards the safe house. "This place isn't that bad. Now let's get inside before we start attracting attention."

I started looking around at my surroundings while Agent Foster escorted me towards the front door. And at that moment was when I noticed Agent Zachary and two other agents had arrived at our location. I swear I wished she'd carry her ass back up north. We didn't need her services down here in Virginia. We would be fine without her needy ass. So, I wished she'd get a life and leave Agent Foster and I alone. Whether she knew it or not, I was going to fuck him before he and I parted ways. And if she wanted a front row seat, I'd personally give her one.

After I managed to block the fact that Agent Zachary was once again in our midst, I looked at the buildings directly across the street from where we were standing. And then I thought to myself, why did he pick this place? The house was situated amongst a few other apartment buildings. And across the street stood a couple more apartment buildings and a small convenient store but there were only a handful of people roaming about. No one stood out like a sore thumb. There were a few people that were senior citizens and they were outside minding their own business so I felt like I was in a safe place. I cracked a smile. "Picture that old couple running up on us with a pistol. That would be a funny ass sight to see." I commented.

Agent Foster turned around and looked at the old man and woman walking side-by-side and said, "Don't sleep on those old people. Those are the ones you would need to worry about."

I laughed. "Yeah, okay. Let them run over here if they want to and I'll personally rip their fucking heads off. And then I'll send them in a gift box to their children."

Agent Rome chuckled and turned his attention towards Agent Foster. "Sounds like she's grown some balls since we left New Jersey." He commented.

Agent Foster smiled. "Yeah, it seems that way doesn't it?"

"Y'all can say what you want to say. But the next time somebody run up on me again like that chick at the hospital, I am going to kill 'em. And I mean that with every fiber of my heart." I warned them.

I figured they believed what I'd just said because neither of them commented. They just looked at each other and continued towards the house. Once we were inside, I sat around in the living room and wondered where my life would take me from here, while they combed through the entire house to make sure the security hadn't been breached. And I had to admit that I was in a fucked up place in my life. How could I go from being a bartender to being a kept chick, living in a plush condo of a high rise and driving a BMW X6 series to staying in this shit hole of a place under witness protection? Did I truly miss something here? I was under the impression that your life was supposed to get better as you get older, not the other way around. I mean, who goes from sugar to shit? I can't keep living under these circumstances and I will let it be known.

Since we left New Jersey in the middle of the night, we arrived here in Virginia around eight a.m. this morning, so I was still a bit tired. I tried falling asleep during the drive but with all the potholes and the friction on highway 95, I found it impossible. I was able to shut my eyes a few times but that was about the gist of it. And after my body realized this, I found a cozy spot on the sofa and made it my resting place. Agent Foster asked me if I wanted to go to one of the bedrooms before I drifted off to sleep, but I told him no and stayed where I was.

I woke up a couple of hours later after I heard screaming from the television set playing in the other room. And when I listened closely and realized that it was the soap operas, I buried my face in the cushion of the sofa. I dreaded the lame ass lines the actresses spoke and the music that followed. This whole thing reminded me of the times Diamond and I used to watch them together. Just imagine how fucked up I was feeling on the inside while listening to the show that was currently playing. I didn't want to wake up to this shit. And to add Diamond to the mix wasn't what I deemed a happy occasion. The last days Diamond and I had together weren't good at all. So, I wanted this bullshit to stop immediately. "Who ever is watching the soap operas need to turn that shit down before I lose my fucking mind." I screamed.

Moments later, Agent Foster entered into the living room. "What's wrong?" he asked.

"Who's watching the television with the volume that loud?" I inquired. The sound of the show was irritating me to death.

Agent Foster smiled. "It's not that loud."

"Yes, the hell it is."

"Well, I'll tell Agent Zachary to turn down the volume."

I sucked my teeth and rolled my eyes when he mentioned Agent Zachary's name. I literally cringed at the sound of it. "Please do before I go and tell her myself." I replied sarcastically.

"She's not the only one in there watching it."

"Please don't tell me you and Agent Rome are in there watching the Young & the Restless too."

"You make it sound so bad."

"That's because it is."

"Me and Agent Rome are just getting in touch with our feminine side."

"Well, why you two are getting in touch with your feminine side would you please turn down the volume?"

"Sure. Why not?" he replied. Before he left the room he wanted to know if I was hungry and if so, what did I have in mind to eat? And after I told him anything would do the trick as long as it was breakfast food, he assured me he'd have one of the agents to go out and have my food back in the next thirty minutes or so. "Think I'll be able to get something on the side?" I asked jokingly.

"Depends on what it is." He commented.

"Why don't you figure it out and get back with me." I replied seductively.

Agent Foster was a smart man. He knew exactly what I was talking about. I just hoped that he'd muster up enough nerves to give me what I want. I'm in desperate need for some dick and he definitely looked like he'd serve me up nicely.

Two days had passed and the boredom had started kicking my ass. Agent Zachary started getting on my nerves too. She made it her business to fuck with Agent Foster while I was around. She knew it bothered me. But, I refused to let her see me sweat.

Other than the drama with Agent Zachary, every one of the FBI agents were leaving the safe house at different times of the day, while I sat around and looked fucking crazy. This house was starting to drive me bananas. At one point the walls started to look like they were closing in on me. And I wasn't feeling this arrangement one bit. I was yearning for a trip outside this house but I knew it was a long shot. I even asked Agent Foster if he'd consider allowing me to go out for tonight's dinner but of course he declined. I was disappointed at his decision and wanted to buck on him and the rules of the protection program. I mean it wasn't like they were doing a good job of protecting me in the first place. And the fact that they had to move me from one safe house to the next was a huge indicator that they couldn't handle this investigation. I say, let me pack up my shit and leave. I'd be better off going into hiding on my own. I would have a better chance of staying off the radar alone than having these niggas around me. They were the ones who brought the heat to me. Their comrades were the ones that sold each other out.

Not me. So, why try to act like you're doing me a favor? All of this crap was bullshit and they knew it.

I believed I bitched to Agent Foster and Agent Rome for forty-five minutes about letting me out for a few minutes to get a breath of fresh air but they wouldn't budge. So, I left well enough alone.

Agent Rome and one of the other agents went out on another food run. This time it was decided that they would be making a trip to the Mexican restaurant Plaza Azteca, which was about five miles away from the safe house. After I gave them my order I headed to the bathroom. Surprisingly one of the agents forgot that they left their I-Phone near the toilet paper ring. My heart fluttered at the sight of it. I fought with the idea of whether or not I should return it to Agent Foster or use it to talk to someone other than Agent Foster and the rest of his fucking clan. I swear I was sick and tired of talking to the same old fucking agents everyday. It was a shame I didn't have any friends or family I liked that I could call. Anybody would do right now. So, as I held the phone in my hand I thought long and hard about who's number I could call. And when I realized that the only person's number I remembered was Devin, I dialed it without hesitation. I figured that if I could just have a few minutes of talk time with Devin I'd be sane again. I needed to hear someone's voice from my hometown. And since Devin was the only person left alive then what were my other options?

"Please let his number be the same." I said quietly as I dialed his number. I pressed the keypad slowly just to make sure no one outside of the bathroom heard it. Immediately after I dialed his cell phone number, I put the phone to my ear and waited for it to ring. And what do you know, it rang. I couldn't believe it. I turned on the water from the sink to distract any sound I made when it was time for me to talk.

"Who dis'?" he answered after the third ring.

I was shocked that the number worked, but I was more shocked after he answered it. "Devin this is Lynise, what's up?" I uttered quietly.

I heard loud music in the background. It sounded like he was in a nightclub. "Who is this?" he asked me once more.

"Devin, it's me, Lynise," I said a little louder trying to talk over the loud music that was playing in the background.

Devin was an old boyfriend. Someone I had a lot of feelings for, but it didn't work out between us. He was a lousy boyfriend. He cheated on me every chance he got, and finally crossed the line after he fucked a stripper at the club I bartended for. After we separated, years later we became cool with one another. And the last time we spoke, he still had feelings for me but I knew I'd never cross that bridge with him again.

"Hey shorty, what's good?" Devin said. I could tell my call surprised him. "Damn, girl, I thought your ass was dead. There have been so many damn rumors about you. From you being in jail, to you being dead, to you running away getting the fuck out of Virginia. It's been crazy out here."

"Who told you I was dead?"

"Everybody's been saying it. But, I'm glad to find out that it's not true. I still love you, you know."

"Yeah, right. You aren't thinking about me. I hear all that loud music in the back. Sounds like you're up to the same tricks." I commented.

"Yeah, you know how I do. The women can't stay off me." He laughed.

"Don't flatter yourself." I said nonchalantly.

"Where you at? In New Jersey now."

"Why you say that?"

"Because you're calling me from a New Jersey number."

"Oh yeah, well this is my friend's number. She's from Jersey. But we're back in the area for a few days so I can show her around a bit."

"Where y'all staying?"

"Well, we're in Newport News now but I won't be here for long." I explained.

"What's in Newport News? You're from this side of the water." He continued to yell through the phone. It sounded like the music was getting louder.

Instead of answering his question, I worked my way towards ending the conversation. I had already been on the phone for more than three minutes. And if Agent Foster found out I was on the phone talking to an outsider, I'd be in big trouble. But before I said my goodbyes, the phone beeped. I pulled it away from my ears and noticed that a call was trying to come through. And the name listed over the number was Agent Zachary, the bitch who plucked my nerves from time to time. I figured Agent Zachary was calling Agent Rome's phone to see if she'd be able to help him locate it. So, I put the phone back to my ear and said a few last words to Devin. "Hey, look I gotta take this other call. But I'll call you before I head back out of town." I told him.

"Tell me where you at so I can come holla at you." He replied.

I knew giving him my location wasn't in the cards for either of us so I gave him a lame ass excuse as to why I couldn't. "I'm staying at someone's place, so I don't think it'll be a good thing to do that." I finally said.

"Well, why don't you come over this side?" he pressed the issue.

"I'll try." I lied. And before I could disconnect the call Agent Foster knocked on the bathroom door and startled the hell out of me.

KNOCK…KNOCK. "Hey Lynise, are you all right in there?" he yelled from the other side of the door.

I took the phone from my ear and muffled the receiver part with my hand and said, "Yeah, I'm fine. What's up?"

"Did you happen to see a cell phone in there? Agent Rome misplaced his so we were hoping he left it in there." Agent Foster said.

"No, I haven't seen a phone in here." I lied again. I was about to piss on myself. It would just be my luck if he didn't believe me and wanted me to open the door for him so he could search me. I would be up shits creek if that happened.

"Okay." Agent Foster replied. I waited for a second or two before I put the phone back up to my ear. I wanted to make sure that he didn't hear me when I said goodbye to Devin.

When I figured the coast was clear and Agent Foster was long gone, I put the phone back up to my ear and when I spoke softly to say hello, Devin was gone. The line was dead because he hung up. Now instead of calling him back, I went into the call log menu and deleted the call I made to Devin. I wasn't about to blow my cover. This was a once in a lifetime opportunity to reach out to the outside world and I took it. I was always told that you can't let the left hand know what the right hand is doing, so I vowed to do just that.

Immediately after I erased Devin's phone number, I stuck the phone down inside my pocket and exited the bathroom. And when I noticed that no one was in sight, I let out a long sigh of relief. It felt good that I didn't get caught.

KEEPING SECRETS

After exiting the bathroom, I knew it would be in my best interest to get rid of the phone. I walked around the entire first floor looking for a good place to put it so it could be found, without giving myself away or shedding any light that I may have had it. So, after carefully mapping out areas around the house, I finally found a spot in the living room area on the floor that Agent Rome could have possibly dropped the phone without knowing it.

I kneeled down to the floor and placed the cell phone by the foot of the sofa. Agent Rome was sitting there before he left, so I felt like this would be the perfect spot to leave it. And as fate would have it, as soon as I placed it down on the floor, Agent Foster walked into the room and literally scared me to death. Luckily I had a chance to get up from the floor before he got a chance to see me near the phone. "Watchcha' doing?" he asked me.

By this time I had taken a seat on the sofa so I was only a few feet away from the phone. I'm sure I looked a little suspicious but I wasn't about to blow my own whistle and tell him I had Agent's Rome's phone the whole time.

"Getting ready to watch something good on the T.V." I finally said. I picked up the remote control from the coffee table in front of me.

Agent Foster took a seat on the recliner near where I had just placed the cell phone. He turned his focus towards the T.V. and that's when it dawned on me that he didn't see me when I hid Agent Rome's phone. Knowing that I was in the clear, I let out a silent sigh of relief.

I sifted through the channels on the television and noticed that the local news was. I sat there to see what was happening in the Tidewater area. The weather segment had already been aired so the news anchor went into a report about serial killer being on the loose. "He's armed and dangerous." The news reporter said.

I started to listen to the rest of the story but I decided against it because it was to depressing. I ended up changing the channel to a reality show. It was Agent Foster's idea to watch it. He said he needed some comic relief especially after everything we've been through. I agreed and we both sat back and watched the show.

Fifteen minutes later, Agent Rome and Zachary entered back into the house with our food in hand. My stomach was growling uncontrollably so I jumped up and grabbed my food as soon as they sat it down. I took my container of enchiladas and my refried beans back into the living room so I could enjoy it while I was watching television.

While I ate away at my food, Agent Rome joined Agent Foster and I. He started looking around for his phone. He searched around every crack and crevice and when he walked over to where I was sitting he finally stumbled upon it. His eyes lit up. "Here it is." He smiled as he picked the phone up from the floor.

Agent Foster looked at Agent Rome puzzled. "That's strange. Because I looked over there and I didn't see it." He said.

"Well, it's here now." Agent Rome said and stuck the phone into the holster attached to the belt area of his pants.

I acted like I was so engrossed in the show that I couldn't comment at all. I was able to look at Agent Foster through my peripheral vision and saw his expression as he watched me. But once again, I didn't entertain it. I was good at pulling the wool over a nigga's eyes so tonight was no different.

WHO SPILLED THE BEANS

"What's up, girlfriend?" I could hear the disdain and hatred in Diamond's words. I understood her hatred against me. I was the one responsible for Bishop and his guys killing her. This was the second time I was having this fucked up dream with her taunting the hell out of me.

"Why are you fucking with me, Diamond? You brought all this shit on yourself. If you would not have been so fucking greedy and sneaky then you wouldn't be in this predicament." I replied, doing my best to let her ass know I didn't like her hounding me in my damn dreams. She was a pain in the ass while she lived, and the only thing that had changed was that she was dead.

"Well bestie for one, I'm bored as hell! And two, you had this shit coming to you. I mean, why else would I be a bitch in your side." Then she laughed. Her laughter was treacherous and gut-wrenching.

"What the fuck is so funny?" I asked her. She was getting on my fucking nerves.

I'm just counting down the days until I see your soul floating around here like everyone else's. It's gonna be home sweet home for you." She smiled like she could see my destiny.

"Bitch, I told you before I will never come here. This is where you belong. Not me. I don't go around fucking every nigga my best friend had. And I don't set my friends up to get murked either, unless they deserved it. See, that's what you're all about. So, kiss my ass bitch and rot in this hell hole!" I screamed. I wanted this bitch to disappear. And I wanted this fucking dream to end.

The one thing I didn't get was Diamond's voice was deep, hoarse and eerily cold. She never was one who had the sweetest or nicest voice but she was scary and it sent chills up my spine. She was my best friend. The one I trusted. I loved Diamond more than I loved any of my relatives. And she betrayed me for a nigga who didn't get a fuck about either one of us. He played both of our dumb asses. She ended up in a pool of her own blood and I found myself on the run for my life. How fucked up was that?

"You're scared aren't you?" she smiled once again.

"Scared of what? Bitch you don't scare me." I spat.

"You're scared because you know you're about to die. Bishop is looking for you. And from what I seen, he's going to find you and butcher you just like he did me. And when he's done killing you, he's going to let you bleed like a fucking pig."

"Shut the fuck up! You don't know what you're talking about. I'm not scared of Bishop. And he ain't gonna do shit to me." I yelled. I was becoming annoyed by the fact that she could be right. I mean, she was dead and I figured that maybe she could actually see what was going to happen to me. But then, I thought about the fact that she could be lying in an effort to scare me. I mean, why would she warn me? She hated me as much as I hated her, so it would behoove her to keep me in the dark. Wasn't that what enemies did?

"I see the wheels in your head are spinning. You don't know what to believe do you? Well, you can walk around here with your head stuck in the clouds but as soon as you come down, one of those agents is going to give your grimy ass up to Bishop. Watch and see.

Hearing Diamond tell me that one of the agents in my midst was going to give me up to Bishop wasn't something I wanted to hear. I wasn't feeling that bullshit at all. So, what was I to do? Take heed or sweep that shit underneath the rug? I needed some answers and I needed them now.

"Who's going to give me up to Bishop? Which agent are you talking about?" I asked Diamond. I figured since she spilled the beans about one of the agents giving me up, then she'd tell me who it was.

"Figure it out yourself." She told me and then she gave me this cunning looking smirk. I knew she had it in for me and nothing would ever change that.

"Fuck you! You evil bitch! I hope you burn in hell forever!" I screamed.

"Hey Lynise, wake up. Are you all right?" Agent Foster asked me.

Startled by his words, I jumped out of my sleep and opened my eyes. It was dark in the room so I could barely see Agent Foster. I blinked my eyes a few times. "Agent Foster is that you?" I asked.

He turned on the light next to the bed I was laying in. I was blinded for a second but I regained my sight a few seconds later.

"Yes, it's me. Are you okay? You're sweating like a dog."

I sat up in the bed and wiped the sweat from my forehead with the back of my hand. "I just had a nightmare and it was crazy."

"Well, you're up now. So, take a deep breath." He instructed me.

I sat on the bed and tried to jog my memory about the shit I had just dreamt. I remembered Diamond was a big part of my dream. And I also remembered her telling me that one of the agents was going to put me on a silver platter and serve my ass up to Bishop. Who was going to do it, she didn't say. But, I knew that I needed to watch my back from this point moving forward because it could be any of these motherfuckers in this house. Everybody was a suspect to me. How I was going to find out who it was? I didn't know. But, I knew I'd better get clever pretty quick.

I started to fill Agent Foster in on the dream I had, but I had become instantly leery of him because he could be the very one Diamond warned me about. So, I decided to keep my mouth closed. "I need to get some water." I said.

"Well, stay put. I'll go get it." He told me and then he left the room.

After he left the bedroom, I sat back and thought to myself how I was going to play out this whole scene. I knew I needed to come up with an escape plan before one of these agents tricked me up. And if I don't do it sooner than later, then I'm gonna be one dead bitch!

WHAT HAVE I DONE NOW?

It was eight thirty-five in the morning and I was lying in the bed. No one knew this but me, but I never went back to sleep after that dream I had with Diamond. To be perfectly honest, I was afraid to go back to sleep for fear that someone was going to come in my room and slice my fucking neck. At this point, I didn't trust anyone. Besides that, the nightmare I had kind of energized me. It prepared me in a way to stay alert so I was somewhat ready for the day even though I stayed in bed.

I was lounging with my back against the headboard when Agent Foster rushed into the room. "Get up right now!" he demanded. I could tell that he was angry.

"Why do I have to get up? What's wrong?" I questioned him.

He grabbed me by my arm and escorted my ass out of bed and onto my feet. "I said, get your ass up right now. You've got some explaining to do." He roared.

"Why? What did I do? And why you grabbing on me like this?" I asked him. I was pissed off by the way he was being rough with me. I wasn't feeling this kind of treatment at all.

"Don't play dumb with me." He screamed. His eyes were red. And they were beaming at me like fire.

Two minutes later Agent Rome entered into the room. He walked in with his arms folded like he was about to reprimand me. And from the look on his face, I already knew why they were here. Some how or another my cover was blown and now they know I reached out to my ex-boyfriend Devin. "Is somebody gonna tell me what this is all about?" I asked, trying to play dumb. I wasn't about to admit what I did until they brought it up first.

"We know you used Agent Rome's cell phone the other night. Now tell us what made you do that? Do you know you put our operation in jeopardy?" Agent Foster roared. He was livid.

I took a seat on the edge of the bed. I wasn't about to allow him to continue to spit little droplets of spit while he was fussing at me. I knew he was angry but it didn't warrant him to yell in my damn ear and saturate my face with his saliva. This was uncalled for.

"Look Foster, what do you want me to say?" I sighed heavily.

"I wanna know why did you use Agent Rome's phone and call that guy?"

"What makes you think I called someone?" I tested him. Once again I was in denial mode. I wasn't about to tell on myself. I mean, who does that?

"Since you want to be a smart ass, let me be the one to tell you that your little boyfriend Mr. Devin is dead." he blurted out.

I gave him this shocked expression. I could feel my eyes swell up in my head. But I didn't utter one word.

Yes, after you called and spoke to him, he was found dead a few hours later. And once the homicide detectives went through his phone records and pulled Agent Rome's phone number out of the list, they contacted us to find out why would the victim be talking to a federal agent? So, we wanna know why you were talking to him."

I was baffled by Devin's sudden death. I couldn't believe what Agent Foster was telling me. Was he just pulling my leg to get me to admit that I had called him? "Is he dead for real?" I wondered aloud.

"Yes, he's dead. Someone shot him in the chest twice." Agent Foster answered me.

"Nah, I don't believe that. I know what you guys are doing." I cracked a smiled. "Y'all are playing games to get me to say that I called him."

Agent Foster leaned over into my face. "Do you think this is a joke? Well, it's not. Mr. Devin Houston is dead and we need to know what you two were discussing when you last spoke to him." He yelled. And I could tell that he was serious. He was very serious. And even though I didn't want to believe what he was saying, something told me that this was not a game and this situation had gone to another level.

I tried to gather my thoughts so I could figure out what I was going to tell Agent Foster and Agent Rome. I knew I had absolutely nothing to do with him getting killed but would they believe me? Another thing that weighed heavily on my mind was that I couldn't tell them that I told Devin I was back in town. They'd go crazy if I let that cat out of the bag. So, I figured the only way to settle their minds was to tell them that Devin was an old boyfriend that I called to check on and that was the gist of it. Maybe they'd believe me and leave well enough alone.

"First off we were on the phone for only about three minutes so we really didn't talk about much." I said and then Agent Foster interjected by saying, "What did you two talk about?"

"Well, we talked about him missing me. And then we talked about where I've been."

"And what did you tell him?" Agent Foster's questions continued.

"I told him I was in New Jersey and that I was chilling with a few of my female friends. And he in turn said he was happy for me. And that was it."

Agent Foster looked at me like he wasn't sure if I'd told him everything. He folded his arms and said, "That's only like a minute and a half of conversation time. You've got another minute and a half left, so I know y'all had to have talked about something other than where you were?"

I thought for another second or two and jogged my memory to see if I had left anything out. I knew what information I was keeping safe to my heart, but would it be wise to tell Agent Foster and Agent Rome that Devin made the comment that he thought I was dead? I figured if I opened that can of worms, there would be more questions.

"Other than telling me he still loved and missed me, that was all we talked about." I finally said.

"That's bullshit! She's lying." Agent Rome blurted out.

I turned and faced Agent Rome, "You don't know me. So, mind your business." I snapped.

"You used my cell phone. And you put us all in danger so this is my business." He snapped back.

"And y'all haven't put me in fucking danger?" I spat. I was getting ready to rip his ass apart, but Agent Foster stopped me.

He tried to press his hand against my mouth but I immediately pushed it away from me. "Shhh! Be quiet. We're not going to get anywhere if we're fussing back and forth."

"Try to shhh....him up. He's the one running his mouth." I yelled.

"Look, let's not deviate from what's important here. There's a guy that's dead and a couple of local homicide detectives want to know what was your relationship to him."

"Well, just tell them that he and I weren't related. But we used to date some years back and that's it. And that I haven't seen him since I left for New Jersey and that's about the sum of it."

"Are you sure that's it?" Agent Foster wanted to know.

"Yes, I'm sure."

"Would you have any information as to who may have wanted to kill him?" Agent Foster asked.

"No, as a matter of fact, I don't. Devin was the type of guy that stayed in his own lane. He was harmless. So, it's puzzling me that he's dead." I explained.

"Well, get dressed because you're gonna have to answer these questions all over again in front of the homicide detectives assigned to this case."

My heart was already beating out of control. But to hear that I was about to go and sit in a fucking room and be interrogated by a couple of police detectives wasn't something I was looking forward to. I was getting sick on the stomach that instant.

"I didn't have anything to do with him getting murdered so why do I have to go and talk to a couple of cops? That just doesn't make any sense to me." I expressed.

"That's besides the point. You may not have had anything to do with him getting shot but the fact is that you talked to him just several hours before he expired. So, the Virginia Beach detectives want to sit down and go over a few questions with you. Every agent in this house will help me escort you to and from the precinct so you'll definitely be safe."

"Why can't they come here?" I asked. I wasn't in any way trying to travel back to Virginia Beach. That place reeked of dead corpses and I wasn't trying to get jammed up in that scene.

"Because we can't risk anyone knowing where we are. It's better if we go to them." Agent Foster insisted.

"But what if we get railroaded again." I pressed the issue. Going to Virginia Beach would open up another can of worms. Running into Detective Whitfield and Detective Rosenberg would compromise everything I've worked for. I was wanted by them and now they're gonna get a chance to see me after all this time and who knows, they may even try to hold me for the murders involving Katrina, Duke & Diamond. What a fucked up position I was in. Geesh!

"Get railroaded by who? Now one even knows that we're here?" Agent Rome interjected.

"Yeah, and no one knew that we were at the other places to and look what happened." I replied sarcastically. I wasn't about to let him beat me down with that nonsense. Agent Rome had no idea what kind of people I used to deal with. Everyone I knew from my former life was grimy and they'd pull the trigger quicker than Bishop would.

"Please do me a favor and shut up!" I snapped once again. Agent Rome was getting on my last nerve. I had now stuck him in the same boat with Agent Zachary. Both of them were officially my enemies. And I wanted nothing to do with them.

"No, I won't shut up! Because it was you that used my cell phone and called that young man and look what that has done."

I sucked my teeth and jumped up from the bed. "I ain't got time for this shit." I said and then I went into the bathroom. After I slammed the door shut, I turned on the shower water so I could drown their voices out. I didn't want to hear another word they had to say. How dare they blame all this shit on me? I wasn't the only one around here who fucked up. They fucked up too. And then to have brought along a dumb bitch like Agent Zachary, so she could upset my world even worse wasn't a good decision on their part. So to hell with all of them and their fucking badges.

Speaking of the dumb bitch, I had only been in the shower for about seven minutes and I got a knock on the bathroom door. I yelled, who is it? So after the bitch announced herself she had the nerve to ask me how much longer I was going to be in there. I started not to answer her, but I did. And after I said, "After I wash my ass," she got the message and carried her worrisome ass back to where ever she came from.

There was no doubt in my mind that she ran back and told Agent Foster what I said. But at this point in the game I didn't care. What could he do to me that hadn't already been done? I figured that if I made it out of all this shit alive, then it would all be worth it.

RAISING HELL

I got dressed and met Agent Foster, Agent Rome and Agent Zachary on the first floor. The other agents were outside in the vehicles waiting for us to join them. After we got into the SUV that was parked a few feet ahead of the SUV parked behind it, Agent Foster went through a checklist to see if everything was in proper order.

Once we were on the road, I started imagining what was going to happen once Detective Whitfield and Rosenberg found out I was back in the picture. It would be devastating if they tried to lock me up. It would be fucked up if they did. So, I hoped for my sake that Agent Foster had enough clout to prevent them from doing anything to me.

I didn't say anything as we hit I-64 East. We passed Christopher Newport College and Hampton University, and suddenly I was getting more nervous than before. The Tidewater area was where I was from. I used to call it home. Now it's considered enemy territory and in a matter of minutes we would be out in the opening and all bets would be off.

"You still have time to tell us what else you and your ex-boyfriend was talking about before he was murdered." Agent Foster said out loud.

I let out a long sigh. "Look, I already told y'all everything we talked about."

"You better not be lying to us." Agent Rome blurted out. "Because if we get to this precinct and find out that you have, we're going to make your life a living hell." He continued. He stared at me through the rearview mirror and his facial expression was menacing.

"Too late. My life is already a living hell. So, you can't do shit to me!" I roared. I was irritated by Agent Rome's voice. I wanted him to shut the fuck up during the duration of this trip to the police station.

Unfortunately for me, he had another agenda. He went into a spiel about how he should've allowed that bitch back at the hospital to take me out of my misery. And then he went on to say how the bureau should not have wasted one penny on me because I was unworthy. I listened to all his bullshit and waited for Agent Foster to chime in and take my side but he didn't. Agent Foster didn't say one word in my defense. So, was he sick of my ass too? Well, if he wasn't then he sure had a fucked up way of showing it.

I thought Agent Zachary was going to throw her two cents in it. But, she didn't. She gave me a few dirty looks like she agreed with everything Agent Rome said. I started to unleash my fury on her ass, but I left well enough alone. I figured I had bigger fish to fry when I arrived at the Virginia Beach precinct.

"Let me know when you're done talking because none of this shit you're saying mean anything to me." I interjected.

"It may not mean anything to you now, but when all of this is over, I hope you find yourself a good hiding place because we won't be protecting you anymore. And we'll hate to hear something happened to you."

"Trust me, you ain't gonna have to worry about me. I'm gonna be fine. So the quicker y'all get this shit over with the quicker I'll be out of your faces. And don't be surprised if you get mirked before I do." I fired back. I had to let this motherfucker know that I wasn't the type of chick that would allow a nigga to talk shit to me and not say anything back to him. I'm from the streets and I've done a lot of shit to keep myself alive. And if it meant to stab someone in the back or take his or her life then so be it.

Agent Rome turned his head around like the exorcist. He looked like he was fucking possessed. "Is that a threat?" he roared.

"It's whatever you want it to be." I responded sarcastically. And then I turned my attention outside of the truck as we continued driving down highway I-64.

"Foster I don't know how you keep putting up with her shit!" Agent Rome roared. "But, if she steps out of line or puts this team in jeopardy one more time then I'm going over your head."

"You ain't gotta wait for me to step out of line!" I spat. "Do whatcha' gotta do now! I ain't scared of you or anyone back at y'all office. So, why don't you call 'em now?"

"Calm down Lynise." Agent Foster interjected as he placed his hand on my left thigh.

"Nah, fuck that! Tell that motherfucker in the front seat to calm down!" I continued. My adrenaline was pumping. And all I wanted to do was go off on everyone around me, including Agent Zachary's dumb ass.

Agent Rome said a few more sarcastic remarks but I ignored him, I turned my focus on what lied ahead. We were on our way to Virginia Beach and I had the slightest clue as to how my visit would turn out. I just hoped that I didn't get crossed up once Detective Rosenberg and Whitfield got me in a room. Police officers weren't shit. And now I'm finding out that FBI agents weren't any better.

THE INTERROGATION ROOM

With Agent Foster, Rome, Zachary and the other two agents heavily guarding me, all of us entered into the 3rd Precinct. I saw a few Narcotic Detectives I knew from around the way. I even saw this nigga I knew named Pierre. Pierre used to be the man back in the day. He used to run a couple of weed spots in Norfolk. All the bitches from the hood used to fight over that cat too. But as fate would have it, he fucked around and started snipping coke. And once his coke habit got too much for his pockets, he fell off the wagon and no body wanted to do business with him anymore. Cats wouldn't front him any weed packages and the chicks cut him off because he didn't have any money. So, it didn't surprise me to see him getting chummy with these crackers. See Pierre was a cokehead who probably got busted with a small quantity of product and got scared when the narcotics detectives told him he'd do five years in the can for it. And when niggas ain't trying to do time, they'd roll over on the next nigga quicker than you'd be able to blink your eyes. And being as though, Pierre knew a lot of hard hitting players in the area that brought in major weight, he had a bargaining chip and a couple of get-out-of-jail free cards. To a snitch, that was like music to their ears.

He was handcuffed to a chair placed next to a desk that I was sure belonged to a narcotics detective. Pierre was sitting there alone but I already knew why he was there. Niggas from the streets only hung around the police when they were trying to cut a deal. And since Pierre knew a lot of what was going on around the Tidewater area, he knew he could write his own ticket. He just better hope that no one else sees him here because he'd find himself in a worse off situation than the one I'm in.

I put my head down while I was being escorted pass Pierre, but he recognized me anyway and made it known to every officer in the place that he knew me. "Hey Lynise, what's up girl?" he blurted out.

I lifted my head back up slowly and smiled at him.

"Whatcha' doing in here?" he kept talking. He seemed like he was high. So, I did everything within my power to ignore him. But it didn't work. "Don't act like you don't know me." He continued.

"I'm doing all right." I finally said.

But that wasn't enough. He wanted more answers from me. "I heard some niggas is looking for you." He blurted out.

"Tell me who isn't." I replied sarcastically and then I turned my attention away from him. I saw Agent Rome look at Pierre from head to toe. And I could tell that he would've loved to sit Pierre in a room and pick him for information, but he knew he was there for another reason and now wasn't the time.

We were finally greeted by two detectives who happened to be Detective Whitfield and Detective Rosenberg. Their faces lit up like a Christmas tree when they saw my face. I can't say I did the same. "Long time no see," Detective Whitfield said first.

"Yes, it has been a long time, huh?" Detective Rosenberg commented.

"Weren't you supposed to help us with the Duke Carrington's case?" Detective Whitfield asked, as if he was trying to refresh his own memory.

"You tell me." I replied nonchalantly. But I knew he was only being a smart ass. He and Detective Rosenberg both knew I was supposed to help them build their case against Duke and that bogus ass doctor he had working with him at that illegal ass adoption agency. I knew everything about the murders of those innocent young girls whose babies they took for their own financial gain. And they knew my testimony would be rock solid if I would've stayed around and gave it to them. Too bad that Duke was dead now, so my testimony wouldn't mean shit.

"Yeah, now that I think about it, you were supposed to help us with that case, along with the murder involving your ex-roommate and a few others.

"Look, I don't remember promising y'all all of that. Now can we get this other shit over with so we can get out of here?" I became snappy. I was ready to walk out on these motherfuckers if they didn't get their shit together in the next few minutes. Whether they knew it or not, my time was precious. And I shut down after a certain time.

"Why sure we can." Whitfield smiled.

After Agent Foster and the rest of the agents shook the detectives hands, we were all escorted into a conference like room. It wasn't one of those two-way mirror interrogation rooms that you'd see on T.V. This room was one of those conference rooms' attorneys' used to have meetings in. In other words it was more laid back than I would have imagined.

While the detectives went through the preliminaries about what I was about to say could be used against me in a court of law, Agent Foster's cell phone started ringing. So, he left the room to answer it. I watched him leave but Detective Whitfield quickly got my attention when he said some other bullshit about if I needed an attorney and couldn't afford one, one could be appointed to me. So, I interjected by saying, "Am I under arrest or something?"

"No, you're not." Detective Whitfield said.

"So, what's up with all the reading my rights and stuff? I know the drill already. So, can we get on with this so I can get out of here?" I said.

"What can you tell us about Devin Houston?" Whitfield didn't hesitate to ask.

"The only thing I can tell you is that he used to be my boyfriend a few years ago and that's about it."

"Why did you two break up?" his questions continued.

"Because I got tired of him fucking around on me with a whole bunch of bitches. A girl can only take but so much."

"How long ago was it that you walked away from the relationship?" Rosenberg chimed in.

"Just a couple of years ago."

"Can you be more specific?" Rosenberg pressed the issue.

"I don't know. Maybe it was twenty-three to twenty-four months ago. I lost count if you wanna know the truth." I replied and rolled my eyes and noticed Agent Foster re-enter the room.

"Well, can you tell us what line of work your ex-boyfriend was into before his death?" Whitfield wanted to know.

"I haven't seen or spoken to him in a while so I can't tell you what he was doing."

"Do you know if he had any enemies?" Rosenberg jumped back in.

"Who doesn't have enemies? I'm sure you have some." I replied sarcastically.

"Just answer the question." Agent Foster interjected. I was shocked that he opened his mouth. I looked back at him and noticed that he had gotten tired of this so-called interrogation already. He must've realized that this whole thing was a complete waste of all our time and wanted me to hurry up and finish this Q & A session as fast as I could.

Without further ado, I answered the detective's questions. All of them. But when he switched up the game and asked me a question about why was my DNA in the apartment at the time Diamond was murdered? I almost shit bricks. I didn't know whether to curse the motherfucker out or play dumb. I mean did he think I was fucking stupid? Did he think I'd make a confession? I hoped not. I'd be signing my life away for a twenty-five year sentence in prison if I told him what I knew. Hell, they'd give my ass charge for being an accessory to murder faster than I could snap my fingers. So, I remained calm and said, "If you would've done your homework you would've found out that Diamond and I used to be roommates. So if my DNA was in the apartment, that was only because I used to live there."

"Ms. Carter we already knew you resided there. But we also know that you brought some men there to murder her. We've got several witnesses who said they saw you and a few men enter inside of the apartment and left about five minutes later. So, don't blow up our asses! We know you know what happened." Detective Rosenberg said.

"You don't know shit! And whoever your so-called witnesses are told you a fucking lie! I wasn't there when she got killed. I wasn't even in the vicinity. So, when you get back on the horn, I want you to tell your witnesses to get their facts straight because I'm the wrong sister." I snapped. And even though I was lying through my teeth, I looked at Rosenberg like I could snap his fucking neck. I couldn't let him make a fool of me in front of everyone. I was a snitch in their eyes. And snitches had bad reps according to law enforcement officers. Snitches weren't to be trusted, so it didn't matter if I denied having anything to do with Duke or Diamond's murder because they'd never believe me. Once I realized that I wasn't going to win this round with Detective Rosenberg, I digressed and turned my attention towards Agent Foster. I needed to see his face. I knew he was thinking all kinds of crazy shit in his head. I knew he was probably thinking that I was some drama magnetic from the hood and every time someone came in contact with me ended up getting killed. As far as

I was concerned, that wasn't a good look on my part. And at this point, I was a walking liability.

"Let me tell you something," Whitfield jumped back in. "There is a rumor that the Carter brothers want you dead. They are convinced that you were the one who killed or had Duke Carrington killed. And to our understanding, there is a one hundred thousand dollar bounty on your head."

What the fuck! I physically turned my body around and looked at Agents Foster and Rome. Both had stern facial expressions. And although Agent Rome's face didn't show it, I knew he was growing more and more disgusted of me. Agent Zachary even looked like she was disgusted. But she kept her mouth closed like everyone else.

I turned back around to face the detectives. "Who told y'all that bullshit?"

"We have a few reliable sources." Whitfield said.

"Well you tell your reliable sources that I didn't do shit to Duke or had anything done to him. So, they need to get their fucking facts straight." I said and then as soon as I closed my mouth we all heard a loud explosion. And then the entire precinct shook. It felt like a fucking earthquake. "Get down!" Agent Foster yelled. And everyone in the conference room hit the floor.

When you live in the 'hood, loud booming noises create one reaction; hit the fucking ground.

I found out a few minutes later that I wasn't the only one who hit the floor. Agent Foster and Agent Rome were immediately by my side, telling me to stay low. Agent Zachary and the other agents did the same. But moments later, Agent Foster and Rome ordered Agent Zachary and one of the other agents to go outside the room to see if there was a way we'd be able to get out of this place in one peace. So, they left.

"Where are y'all going?" Detective Whitfield asked Agent Zachary and the other agent as he pulled his gun from his holster. He and Detective Rosenberg were also on the ground taking cover.

"They're going out there to see if there is another way we can get out of here," Agent Rome stated.

As soon as the words came out of his mouth, we heard gunshots ringing out throughout the building. The Third Precinct was a one-story building. This place was huge and it had plenty of hallways and rooms. I didn't know what was up, but I figured whatever it was had to be some insane mercenaries. I mean, who was bold enough to bomb a fucking police precinct?

The shooting was non-stop and that was understandable if the precinct was under attack, which evidently it was. Bad guys shooting and police returning fire. This whole attack was so fucked up on so many levels.

The conference room had two doors on the same side of the room, about thirty feet from each other. When the first door opened, suddenly I saw the two agents and two detectives weapons turned towards the door as if on instinct.

"Don't shoot!" Agent Zachary stated. "It's only me and Agent Carr."

"What the fuck is happening out there?" Agent Foster asked them.

"Someone threw several grenades through the front door and they went off." Agent Zachary answered. She was panting as if she was out of breath. "And there's at least five or six gunmen that I counted emptying out their arsenal on every police officer they see." She continued. She wasn't the confident Agent Zachary I first met. This person I was seeing now looked spooked. She acted like she was out of her element.

"How far are they from this room?" Agent Foster asked.

"If we get out of here now, we'll have at least a two minute head start on them." She told him.

"Is there a back way out of this building," Agent Foster asked the detectives.

"Yeah, but there are a lot of hallways in this fucking building," Agent Whitfield responded. "The best way is to just keep heading back towards the back and watch out for the hallways that lead back to the front of the building."

"In other words, you guys are saying that if we don't watch our asses, we could still get blown away?" I replied.

Before he or Detective Rosenberg could respond, Agent Foster shook his head and then he grabbed my arm and said, "Time to move, let's get out of here."

Agent Zachary was the first out the door since she was the closest to it. Agent Foster and I were next, and then Agent Rome and the other agents followed. I was scared shitless when I heard the gunshots and people screaming and yelling.

Before we could hit the next hallway, three guys came around the corner and before they could let off one shot, Agent Foster pushed me to the floor and every agent with us fired their weapons simultaneously. A couple of minutes later, Detective Rosenberg and Whitfield came out of the conference room and fired shots of their own. "They have on flak vests," Detective Whitfield screamed at us. "Shoot them in the face or below the groin if you can."

Finally all three guys were gunned down. Blood covered their entire bodies. So it was a gruesome sight.

"Come on, let's get out of here!" Agent Rome yelled. In uniformed order, all of us scrambled down the long hallway that led to another hallway that finally led to the back door of the precinct.

As we approached the back door two more shooters shot around the corner and started gunning at us like we were in a war. "Kick the door open!" Agent Foster yelled. While Agent Zachary kicked at the door, the other agents started firing another set of rounds at the men who were pursuing us. Miraculously we made it out the back door before any of us were hit.

"Hurry up and close the door!" Agent Rome shouted. This shit was wild. And for various reasons I couldn't get a grip on the things around me. It seemed like everywhere we turned there was shear chaos. Everything was moving so fast that I couldn't keep up. "We gotta call back up?" Agent Zachary yelled.

"Let's get out of here first." Agent Foster told her.

Now I can't say exactly how we got back to the SUV's as quickly as we did, but I can say that I said a silent prayer to God and nearly pleaded with Him to help us. I figured that if He hadn't helped us then we'd surely be dead by now. "Zachary let Agent Carr take the wheel. Rome you come with us." Agent Foster instructed.

One by one all the agents followed Agent Foster's orders and climbed back into the trucks. Engines were revved up and then we sped off like Nascar drivers. "Agents take cover." Agent Foster yelled from the window. "Lynise, you get down on the floor," he continued as we fled the scene.

The moment had arrived after we bolted out of the underground tunnel. It seemed like every thug in the area had the precinct surrounded. Niggas dressed in black were coming from all angles and they were busting shots at us like it was the 4th of July.

Pop! Pop! Pop! Ping! Ping! Ping! Sounds of bullets hitting the SUV rattled my brain. If we hadn't had bulletproof windows we'd be in a world of trouble. "They're shooting at us!" I yelled from the floor of the SUV. I couldn't see anything. But I heard enough to know what was going on.

"Just stay down on the floor." Agent Foster yelled back.

"Please get us out of here." I cried out. I was terrified to no end.

"We got this. You just stay down." Agent Foster told me.

While I rested on the floor of the truck I wondered if we'd get out of this situation alive. But before I could psych myself out to believe that we'd be all right, a very dark picture of myself crossed my mind. And in this dark picture was me lying in a casket. The very people that were pursuing us had killed me. My body was riddled with over a dozen bullets. And the crazy part about all of this was that when I pictured how my funeral would be, only two people showed up. The first person was my mother. And the second person was my sister. That was it. My so-called friends disappeared on me. What a fucked up ending that was.

Realizing how my life could end up, I snapped back into reality. I figured if I didn't want to end up dead then certain things needed to happen. I lifted my head up over the headrest and noticed that we had gotten a ways from the precinct. In fact, we had just veered onto the highway and we were going east, which meant we were in route to go back to Newport News. But not too far behind us were two cars tailing us. And they were hot on our asses.

WE GOT MORE ACTION

Agent Rome was driving our vehicle like he was Dale Earnhardt Jr. himself. He maneuvered this truck in and out of the steady flow of traffic with ease. Sorry to say that his driving techniques didn't stop the gunmen from firing their weapons at us. Pop! Pop! Pop! Ping! Ping! Ping! My body flinched with each bullet that hit the truck. I was shaking and I really was scared as hell. This highway chase seemed like it would never end. "Father God, please let us get back to our house safely." I cried out. My heart was pumping with fear.

I looked directly behind us and saw that Agent Carr was trying to run both of the cars containing the gunmen off the road. I even noticed Agent Zachary firing her handgun at them in hopes she'd be able to stop them in their tracks. This was some real life cops and robber's type of shit.

As we merged on the exit to I-64 West, Agent Foster spoke into his Bluetooth, "Let's put some more speed to this, I see three more cars coming up on our asses."

I looked out the back window and realized that Agent foster was right. There were two black SUV's and a white

Cadillac sedan coming in our direction. And they were gaining ground pretty quickly.

"Lynise, get your ass back on the floor," Agent Foster instructed. Before I did just that, I saw the speedometer and Agent Rome was already driving over 100 miles per hour.

Seconds later, more loud, popping and pinging sounds bounced off the windows around us. "What the fuck! Are they gonna run out of bullets any time soon?" I said after I noticed bullets were still being fired in our direction. My heart began to race with every second that passed. It seemed like every time I look up there's an attempt on my life. How much bad karma can a girl take?

Luckily the vehicle we were in had bulletproof windows and thank God they were working. "They're still on our asses!" I screamed. I wanted to live and if I had to watch our backs until we got to safety then so be it.

"Lynise, I said get down on the floor." Agent Foster yelled.

But I couldn't help myself, I felt like I had to do something other than hide on the floor. I mean it wasn't like the bullets were going to penetrate the vehicle we were in so, we weren't in any immediate danger. Or were we? I guessed I spoke to fast because as soon as I blinked my eyes, I saw an SUV in each lane with shooters hanging out of windows firing their guns at our tires. And that's when I became really worried.

"They're aiming at our tires." I yelled.

But my words fell on deaf ears. Agent Rome and Agent Foster were yelling back at one another while Agent Foster was giving the other agents instruction via Bluetooth. It was a bunch of chaos. I just prayed that God would once again get us out of here.

Doing over one hundred miles per hour down highway I-64 was becoming more dangerous by the second. A few cars crashed into each other while we forced our way ahead.

"As soon as we get through the tunnel, I want us to make a stand," Agent Foster said.

I didn't know what else was about to go down but it sounded like we were in for a battle. The tunnel was directly in front of us and it was right before the bridge that connected to Hampton. And as soon as we exited the tunnel, all hell broke loose.

I saw a tall, handsome Latino, sporting dark sunglasses with his hair pulled back into a ponytail. The fucking guy had a bazooka in his hands and aimed directly at us. He pulled the trigger and I knew we were dead, but suddenly Agent Rome veered left and the blast passed us and hit the SUV directly behind us. The impact was deadly, I was sure. Meanwhile, we had done a complete three hundred and sixty degree turn, probably two times, before we finally stopped. Agents Rome and Foster jumped out of the car and joined the Latino and Agent Zachary and Carr. Agent Foster had told me to get out of the car and hide behind one of the cars. There was another black SUV and I could only assume it was the Latino's ride.

I hid behind one of the SUVs and I looked, as all five agents were loaded for bear with some serious weapons. All of them had assault rifles and handguns. The blast had taken out one SUV and the white sedan had run into the back of that vehicle. I thought this was it as the agents moved in with their guns pointed at the other SUV. There were no way the guys in that SUV were going to put up a fight. Shit, I was completely wrong.

The four doors of the SUV opened simultaneously as if they were synchronized. And four guys, two blacks, a white and an Asian came out blazing, but this was the shortest firefight in the history of firefights. It was as if every agent had selected their own gunmen to kill. The four assholes went down fast. Hell, from what I saw, two of them were even shot in the head. And all of this shit was happening on I-64 in the middle of the damn day. How fucking crazy was this? Shit, this had to be a dream!

Then Agent Foster and his guys moved in closer and surveyed their damage as well as see if anyone was still living. As they got closer to the burning SUV, two doors on the white sedan opened and no one came out. I noticed that Agent Foster and Agent Carr were closing in on the sedan. No one came rushing out of the car like they did in the SUV. I guess seeing four of your partners get shot had a tendency to make people change their mind about coming out blasting guns.

Three other vehicles came rolling in. Shit, now I was really scared because all of the agents were near the mouth of the tunnel and I was left alone. I was happy when I saw the guy get out of the truck with an FBI jacket on. But I still hurriedly made my way towards Agent Foster and his crew. At that moment, I didn't trust anyone except Agent Foster. Even though they were still engaged in battle, I still preferred to take my chances with him.

I got close to their operation. I heard car doors opening and closing and rushing footsteps towards the scene.

When I looked around, I noticed that five local agents and at least seven cop cars had arrived on the scene.

What was so crazy was that one of those agents grabbed my arm and said he had to get me out of here. I verbally objected and I guess that was enough to distract Agent Carr, as he looked in our direction, and then seconds later I heard a shot and Agent Carr went down.

Several feet away from me, Agent Foster and Rome shot multiple rounds at the driver of a white sedan and they literally blew half the man's head off. It was another gruesome fucking scene. It was so fucking gruesome, I nearly vomited on the shoes of the agent who had grabbed my arm.

Then I heard Agent Foster say, "Step out of the vehicle now or your ass is dead." As I was recovering and wiping my mouth, the guy in the back seat of the car came out with his hands up. The only thing, it wasn't a man. It was a fucking woman. And I knew the bitch. Her name was Gina. She was a stone, cold bitch that used to do odd jobs for Neeko when he needed someone roughed up. She was only five seven, maybe five eight, and slender like a runway model, but the word out on the streets was that the bitch knew ten types of karate, taekwondo and jiu-jitsu. Plus, I heard she was deadly as hell with a knife and was an expert shooter on at least twenty different guns. She was a treacherous bitch to say the least.

The initial thing that scared the hell out of me was that she was indeed one of the most notorious killers in the Virginia area and for her to have a group of niggas hunting me down in broad daylight, on a congested highway, where there was a ton of witnesses, meant that this shit was really serious. I guessed what Detective Rosenberg and Whitfield said was true. There was a bounty out on me.

THERE'S ONLY ONE BITCH IN THIS CLIQUE

Agent Carr was all right. His flak vest saved him. Agent Rome and one other agent had killed the guy that shot Agent Carr. As far as the other causalities, Agent Foster, Rome and Zachary killed ten of the eleven motherfuckers sent to kill me. The only one who had survived was Gina, the apparent leader of the group.

And the most fucked up thing about all of this was traffic at the tunnel was shut down for three hours and we were still at the scene. A scene that now included cop cars, ambulances, fire trucks and of course, the FBI. As much as the other agents wanted to get me away from the scene, I wouldn't go anywhere without Agent Foster. I was not about to let him out of my sight.

"All right bitch, start talking," Agent Foster said to Gina.

Gina looked at me, then at Foster with a sneer on her face. "Fuck you," the chick said. And as soon as the words came out of her mouth, Agent Rome threw a straight right hand to her jaw. Damn, he hit her so hard it hurt me. And Agent Foster followed this up with a quick bolt of juice from the Taser he had. What the fuck, this was torture in the middle of a fucking crime scene with almost a hundred people on the fucking scene.

"Let's try this again, bitch, start talking," Agent Foster said.

"F . . . F . . . fuck—"

Before she could get the "you" out, Agent Foster hit her with another bolt of juice from the Taser. This time he did it for several seconds. Tears were flowing from Gina's eyes. Even though she was trying to kill me, I felt a little sadness for the bitch.

"Talk, Ms. Payne," Agent Rome said. Damn, his voice sounded silky fucking smooth. This nigga had just enough bass in his voice to make a woman wet her panties.

"What . . . you . . . want . . . to know," Gina managed to say.

"Who sent you and how did much they pay you and your bunch to kill Ms. Carter," Agent Foster said.

"What . . . do . . . I . . . get in return," Gina struggled to get the words out. Regardless of how bad she was or how physically fit she was, that Taser Agent Foster was using was no joke. Plus, if her jaw wasn't broke from Agent Rome's hit, then it was definitely sore. Blood was oozing from her mouth by the handfuls.

"You get to live and spend time in a nice prison away from Virginia," Agent Rome stated.

"Shit, motherfucker, I think you broke my jaw," Gina said. Her delivery was slow and deliberate. I don't think it was on purpose. I think her jaw really was fucked up. "That shit doesn't work for me. I have two kids that live in Richmond with my mother. Get my kids and mother and give them new identities and move them to Oregon or Canada some damn where and I will tell you what you want to know."

"We can definitely do that, but we're gonna need you to start talking now," Agent Foster said.

"No, you gotta make sure my family is safe first, then I talk," Gina tried negotiating.

"Sorry, but it doesn't work like that, Ms. Payne," Agent Foster responded. "I'm a man of my word, you can write their information down now and I will put this in motion now, but I'm not doing shit without you telling me what I want to know and telling me now. You understand that? And if you are worried about your family that means whoever hired you knows about your family."

"You're not that big of a bastard to let my family die," Gina stated with a half-ass smile on her face.

"Try me," Agent Foster answered.

"Gina, I hate to admit it but Agent Foster will help you, so tell him what you know." I intervened. "Believe me, those cats you're working for don't give a damn about you! They will feed your mother and your kids to a pack of hungry dogs. So, please don't be stupid. These are your kids and your mom."

Gina looked at me. I was surprised. I thought she would have evil or hatred in her eyes, but they were soft. I realized then that she was thinking about her kids.

"So you are working for Bishop?" Agent Foster asked with a weird look on his face.

"Hell nah! I would never work for that psycho motherfucker." Even I smiled at Gina's comment. It was kind of funny to think she had scruples. "Give me some paper so I can write down my family's information. I want them picked up now."

Gina's hands were handcuffed with her hands in front of her versus being handcuffed with her hands behind her back. Agent Foster gave her paper and she wrote down her folks' information and when she was done she gave the paper back to him. Immediately after taking the information into his hands, he looked at it. Moments later, he opened the door and said a few words to Agent Rome. Agent Rome in turn called another agent over and the deal looked like it was in motion.

"Who hired you?" Agent Foster turned his focus back to Gina.

"The Carter brothers," Gina answered.

"How much they pay you and your crew?"

"Why is that important?" Gina asked back.

"Because that tells me what we are dealing with," Agent Rome explained. "And something tells me if you are worried about your family, the Carters spent a plenty penny for this job."

Gina looked at me again. "Yes they did," she stated. "Evidently, Lynise, they really want you dead. They told everyone of us that we're gonna get paid two hundred grand each to handle this shit."

"What?! Two hundred thousand dollars!" I screamed. "Why?! I don't know shit. I don't know a goddamn thing about the Carter brothers. Why in the fuck do they want me dead?"

Gina started laughing at me. That pissed me off. "What's so fucking funny, bitch?" I spat.

"You are, trick. You really don't know why they want your stupid ass dead. Duke Carrington brought them in five to ten million dollars a fucking month. Their legitimate businesses didn't bring in that type of revenue. And you fucked all of that up when you had Duke disappear."

I didn't say anything. I looked at Agent Foster who was still looking at Gina. I knew for sure now that he wondered what type of chick I really was. I played the game to him like I was some good girl that happened to run into a fucked up situation when I started fucking Bishop. But now, he knows that I'm just as treacherous as this other bitch sitting before us.

Believe me when I say that I wanted to stuff her fucking mouth with a gag. She has talked too much now. And I wanted her to stop this very second. "You don't know what the fuck you're talking about. So, you need to shut your fucking mouth." I continued. I was seething. Granted, I knew I'd fucked up but why let the world know it. And instead of wanting Duke to pay, I should have kept it moving and left the fucking area then. Then after that ordeal, I should have said the hell with Bishop. Now I was in a vicious circle trying to save my life, trying to make it through another day, another week and another month. This was not the life I wanted for myself. Always looking over my head.

"Calm down ladies! This isn't necessary." Agent Foster chimed in. He sounded like he was irritated with us.

"I was only giving you the information he asked me for." Gina said sarcastically and then she gave me a half smile.

"No, bitch, you're being messy. And you don't know what you're talking about." I replied. This bitch was really getting underneath my skin. I wished Agent Foster would give me ten minutes alone with this tramp and I'd shut her up for good.

Gina sucked her teeth. "I don't have time for this shit. So, can y'all get me away from her?" Gina asked.

"We are not through with you yet, Ms. Payne, we need more information," Agent Foster said. "We are taking you to a local office in the Norfolk area for further questioning. So, get her out of here Agent Zachary."

As she was sliding out the SUV, Gina completely fucked me up with her lasting statement to me. "By the way, Lynise, I just want you to know that you're on borrowed time."

She was laughing loud as she departed the car. And I was sure she was laughing at how stupid I was. First I got wrapped up with Duke, then Bishop and now it's the fucking Carter brothers. Who will it be next? Was I walking around with a sign on my forehead giving niggas permission to take my ass out? If I wasn't, then what could it be?

I realized then that this would be a fight to the end. Bishop was on one side, while the Carters were on the other side and my stupid ass was smack dab in the middle.

I wondered if my FBI protection could really do just that—protect me.

STRESS RELIEVER

Two hundred thousand dollars for each hit man. I mean, was it that fucking serious? Well, the Carter brothers thought it was. And it seemed like the more and more I thought about it, the more I got sick to my stomach. I truly regret the day Duke came in my life. He has caused me more stress and heartache dead than he had when he was alive. He was the bad penny, the bad luck that kept giving and giving. Not only that, I was the one who would be looking over my shoulder for the rest of my days.

I remembered Gina coming into the club and sometimes she would be talkative and other times she could be a royal bitch. Neeko would always joke about how he didn't know if she was on her period or bipolar. She was a mess then and from what I could tell, nothing has changed.

After we left the I-64 crime scene, we went to an office building in downtown Hampton where they tried questioning Gina again. She didn't give up anything relevant, just the same old shit. Hell, she was just happy the FBI had rescued her family and put them in witness protection. But that wasn't a done deal until she actually gave them something relevant.

I couldn't sleep. I fell asleep early, probably around nine o'clock. By midnight, I was awake and just lying in bed. I had too much on my mind and my thoughts were anything except organized. I needed something to take my mind off this craziness I was going through. If just for a minute or two would be nice.

I noticed Agent Foster had the same problem I had. He couldn't sleep. Since I had been awake, Agent Foster had been tossing and turning the whole time. I didn't say anything. I didn't know if his nerves were on edge because of everything we'd been through or if he was tired of sleeping on a sofa. When he got up to go to the bathroom, I think my mind went into overdrive. Overdrive with thoughts I had been having ever since I met Mr. Foster.

Sometimes you have to say fuck it and shoot your best shot. That was exactly what I was about to do—shoot my best shot. I didn't know if the bathroom door was locked or not, or if Agent Foster was doing number one or two. I just knew I had to try.

I turned the knob and the door opened. He was taking a leak and turned his head when I came in. It was a good piss because he couldn't stop mid-stream. Damn, I was flabbergasted when I saw that piece of meat. Fuck, it was thick and had to be at least six inches soft. Shit, I could only imagine how big it would be hard.

I was surprised. Agent Foster didn't react or overreact. "I'll be through in a minute," he said.

"Take your time," I said in return.

He smiled. "You like what you see?" he replied as he put his dick back in his running shorts. He washed his hands and I was still at the door. I didn't say anything. "What's on your mind? You knew I was in here, so what's up?"

"I wanted to apologize to you for putting you and the other agents in jeopardy when I reached out to my ex-boyfriend. I figured that if I hadn't used Agent Rome's cell phone called him, then we wouldn't have gone and talked to those homicide detectives and Agent Carr wouldn't have gotten shot."

"I appreciate you saying this. But, you're gonna need to tell the other agents the same thing you're telling me."

"Okay, I will. But, before I do that give me a chance to show you how much I appreciate the many times you've put your life on the line for me."

He smiled again. "I'm waiting," he said.

After Agent Foster gave me the green light I got excited because I was horny as hell. I thought of many ways I could seduce him. But after seeing how big his dick was I knew I couldn't waste a lot of time. My pussy started throbbing. Hell, my pussy was already wet.

He put both his hands on my waist and I know he was about to lift me up and move me. But I grabbed his right hand and guided it to my wet pussy. "You like that," I said after his fingers felt my wet pussy. He didn't say anything. Instead, he surprised me again by finger fucking me. I hadn't realized how fat his fingers were until he stuck one then two up my pussy.

"Oooo, shit," I said as I leaned on the bathroom door. His fingers felt damn good. And like his dick, they were fat as hell. I had on loose shorts myself with thong panties, plus I had on a half tee shirt.

Agent Foster was now taking advantage of my wardrobe, or lack of wardrobe, and kissing my neck and my cleavage area. Then he fucked me up when he pulled his two fingers out of his pussy and stuck them in his mouth. What the ... Then he slipped the strings of my tee shirt over my shoulders and it fell down my body. Then he flicked his tongue on my left nipple. I don't know how long he did that, but it felt good him fingering me while teasing me with his tongue. I was moaning. Enjoying the moment. Then his big lips encompassed my nipple and the way he sucked my nipple was unbelievable.

We did this for at least five minutes or more before he finally start sliding down my body. When he pulled my shorts and panties off, my anticipation was high. When he flicked his tongue on my clit and start eating my pussy, I was in bliss. Agent Foster was on his knees and I was still standing with my left leg over his shoulder. He was eating my pussy and finger fucking me at the same time. This shit was unbelievable. I was getting my pussy ate by a damn FBI agent.

Moments later, he shoved one of his fingers inside my asshole. He went back and forth from eating my pussy to tongue fucking me in my ass. It felt like I was in sex heaven. And I when I felt the power punch of my orgasm I nearly scream with shear ecstasy. I was trying my best not to make too much noise because I didn't want Agent Rome to hear us. But I was hoping that Agent Zachary would get an earful. Allowing her to eavesdrop while Agent Foster fuck me to death would be the highlight of my life. I needed her to know that I was the Queen Bitch around here. Not her.

As Agent Foster continued to eat my pussy, my knees grew weaker by the minute. I felt like I was in heaven. Both of my hands were on the back of his head, pushing his face deeper into my groin, pushing his tongue deeper into my pussy. He had removed his finger from my pussy and now he was tongue fucking me. I couldn't believe it, I was about to come again. This was feeling too damn good.

After my two orgasms, I was happy to trade positions with Agent Foster. My legs were weak, as shit and I didn't mind getting down on knees and handling that huge piece of meat he had between his legs. I was surprised his dick wasn't already hard. But when I started sucking on the head, his dick started getting harder. I didn't know if I could get that dick completely in my mouth. Just sucking on the head was stretching my fucking mouth. Damn, his shit was huge.

I had to concentrate. I took my time trying to work his dick. His dick had grown from six inches soft to about eight or nine inches hard. He ate pussy better than Bishop and I thought that was virtually impossible. Now I wondered if he laid pipe better than Bishop. Hell, his dick was as big as a damn pipe.

I had finally worked that dick and was getting at least a third or half of his dick in my mouth. I was proud of myself. I was doing that the damn thing. Agent Foster's hand was on the back of my head. I looked up and his eyes were closed. He made it no secret how much he loved what I was doing to him. This was good. No! Fuck that. This was great.

His hips was gyrating and pumping my face like he was a man possessed. I wanted his ass to come like he made me come. This shit was excellent. I was sucking Agent Foster's dick like I had never sucked a dick before.

I could feel the energy of his dick rising. I had his ass on the edge when the damnedest thing happened . . . Agent Foster's phone started ringing. Shit! Shit! Shit!

He pushed me back as gentle as he could. Then he rushed out of the bathroom and grabbed the phone.

My first thought was this couldn't be good. Especially at one o'clock at night.

KEEPING SHIT TOGETHER

The phone call wasn't serious so, I thought we'd get back into the swing of things but we didn't. I asked him if everything was all right? And he told me that they were but his mood told me a different story. I couldn't explain the mood swing but whatever it was, it definitely put a damper on our extra curricular activities. In just a snap of the finger, he went right back into work mode. And seeing this made me feel stupid as hell. Who get's their dick sucked and then stop right in the middle of it, only to answer your cell phone and then when you finish your call, you zip up your pants and act like nothing happened. I mean come on you're making me feel like a cheap whore. I almost got lockjaw and now you're zipping up your pants and acting like nothing ever happened is a fucked up way of saying thank you. What a smack in the face.

I think for Agent Foster, I had become more of a piece of ass. I knew he couldn't take me serious even if he wanted to. We were definitely from two different worlds. And I know I wasn't the type chick he was used to dealing with, but I knew he liked the challenge I presented to him.

Yes, I was supposed to be off limits. But I've got needs and if he wanted to be the one to give them to me, then I'm going to leave myself open to that.

Well after my supply of satisfaction was cut off, I decided to head down stairs to the kitchen. Yesterday was a trying day for all of us. After we got ambushed inside of the precinct and while we were traveling back to this house, I took a couple of pills and unwind. It was told to me that they weren't taking me out of the safe house anymore and I was happy about that decision. Now I can concentrate on where I'm going after all of this is over, since I'm wanted in two different states.

"What's for breakfast?" I asked the moment I entered into the kitchen. With all the exercise I got from sucking on Agent Foster's dick, I needed to put something on my stomach.

Agent Rome and Agent Zachary were cooking their poor little hearts out while Agent Foster was sitting at the kitchen table reading the local newspaper. I smelled turkey bacon and turkey sausages, along with some scrambled eggs and toast. "We've got a buffet of food," Agent Rome told me, while Agent Zachary rolled her eyes. I could tell that she wasn't at all pleased to see me. And the first thing that popped in my mind was that she knew about Agent Foster and I fucking the night before. And boy was I happy about that.

I had an edge over her and I was going to use it to my advantage. I knew she wanted something that I had so I planned to flaunt my pretty little self around just like she did when I first met her silly ass. They say it isn't fun when the rabbit got the gun.

"Want me to make you a plate?" she finally opened her mouth. She gave me this menacing look so I didn't hesitate to tell her no.

"Everything smells so good, but I'm really not that hungry so I'm gonna get a glass of juice for right now." I replied as I made my way towards the refrigerator. I was not about to let that bitch stick some poison in my food. Hell no! I'll pass.

"They've made so much food so you should get a plate." Agent Foster chimed in. Yeah, it would be kind of rude not to eat after we made enough to feed a whole army," he continued.

As much as I wanted to eat a plate of that food I wasn't about to play myself. Whether Agent Foster realized it or not, Agent Zachary wasn't feeling me right now. So, I needed to play my position. I wasn't starving so I'd be okay.

"I'll eat later," I said once more and then I grabbed the orange juice from the refrigerator. I retrieved a glass from the cabinet over the sink and poured myself a glass of orange juice. I took a sip from my glass and leaned back against the counter. I looked around at everyone in the kitchen. "Since you guys cooked so much food, why don't you call the other agents to join us so they can eat?" I asked trying to make small talk.

Agent Rome spoke first. "Because they have to stay at their post. We can't have a crew of bandits catching us with our pants down again."

"You never stopped them before." I commented.

"Do you remember leaving out of the hospital without having your neck separated from your head? I mean, I do recall saving you from getting injecting by a lethal dose of serum the nurse's assistant tried to pump into your veins."

"I remember that too. But guess what? Y'all dropped the ball a couple of times after that." I made known. And I looked around the kitchen at Agent Foster, Zachary and Rome when I made my point.

"If you weren't involved with so many people getting killed then you wouldn't be in this situation right now." Agent Rome struck back. I had to admit that he hit me below the belt with that one.

"You can believe what you want, but I know what I did. And it didn't involve me having anybody getting killed. Worry about what Bishop did to his fucking sister and his other girl friend because you really don't know shit about me." I snapped. I was offended by his words. How dare he talk shit to me when he knew nothing about me? Yes, Detective Rosenberg and Whitfield threw a bunch of salt on me back at the precinct, but at the end of the day, they didn't have any proof. If they did, then I would be in their custody right now. And since I'm not, everybody in here can go fuck themselves.

"I know more than you know." Agent Rome blurted out.

"All right you two. That's enough." Agent Foster said after he laid down the newspaper. "We've got more important things to discuss. So, later with the cat and mouse games." He continued as he looked back and forth at Agent Rome and myself.

I knew I hadn't planned to say another word so I left the container of orange juice on the countertop and walked out of the kitchen with my glass of orange juice in hand.

PUBLIC ENEMY NO. #1

After that episode of bullshit that went down in the kitchen, I carried my ass into the living room area to watch a little bit of T.V. I sat the glass of orange juice on the coffee table in front of me. A few minutes later, Agent Foster joined me. He took a seat on the sofa next to me and gave me an earful. "I hear we're closing in on Bishop's whereabouts." He started off saying.

My heart skipped a beat. Hearing that Bishop was about to be arrested was the best news in the world. I figured that when he's gone then all I had to worry about was the Carter brothers. But if I ran off to LA or Seattle Washington somewhere, then they'd never be able to find me and I wouldn't need to be in Witness Protection anymore. This was good new. "So, when will he get arrested?" I wanted to know. I was very anxious for him to answer my question.

"Well, we got word that he's hiding out in a beach house near Hoboken. An agent friend of mine says that he saw him hanging out on the balcony for a few minutes while speaking to someone on his cell phone." He started to explain but I cut him off.

"If they saw him then why hasn't he been arrested?" I asked. I was beginning to get frustrated.

"Lynise, we can't just rush into the house not knowing what we're up against. We've got to do this thing right if we want to bring him in." Agent Foster said.

"So, when do they plan to go in?" I pressed the issue.

"In the next day or so. We're mapping out some things now." Agent Foster said confidently.

"So, what are we going to do now?"

"All we can do is wait."

"What's going on with the Gina chick? Did y'all cut a deal with her?"

"No, as a matter of fact we didn't. After we took her to the local FBI headquarters, she told us she had a change of heart. So, looks like we're on our own again."

"So, what's gonna happen to her?"

"Agent Zachary helped the local agents to process her into the system. So, it looks like she's going to be charged with attempted murder on a federal agent, firing a weapon in an occupying dwelling, among other things. Let's just say that she's never gonna see daylight again."

"What's gonna happen to her family?"

"If she doesn't care about them. Then why should we?"

I picked up my glass of orange juice from the table and looked at it. "You see the pulp swimming around?" I pointed out.

"Yes, what about it?"

"That's me trying to find my way around in all of this bullshit called life. I'm alone in this world. And to keep myself from being swallowed up, I'm gonna have to stand my ground."

"I guess that's what we all have to do. But sometimes all of us aren't to fortunate." Agent Foster said nonchalantly.

"Whatcha' mean by that?" I asked.

"My supervisor Joyce was killed."

"When?"

"Remember when I got that call back at the precinct?"

"Yeah,"

"Well, that's when I found out."

"Why are you just now telling me?"

"Because I didn't feel like it was a good time."

"And now it is?"

"Look, it's done. All right? She's dead." Agent Foster boomed. And then he turned his attention towards the television.

"Bishop did it, didn't he?"

Agent Foster let out a loud sigh. "Yeah, he did. And we got the evidence to prove it."

I stood up from the chair because I could no longer sit down. "How many people is he going to kill before he's able to get to me?" I said aloud. "Does the other agents know about this?" I continued.

"Yes, they do. Everyone knows."

I began to panic. "Oh my God! Y'all are gonna have to do something. I can't sit up in here and act like everything is cool. We need to find somewhere else for me to go."

Agent Foster stood up and grabbed me in a bear hug. "You need to calm down. And have a seat."

"For what? We gotta get out of here. I'm tired of sitting around waiting for someone else to pull out a gun on me. Do you know how it feels to be in constant fear? I'm about to lose my fucking mind!" I yelled.

"Lynise, we can not move you right now. We gotta wait for orders." He yelled.

Finally after playing tug-a-war with me, Agent Foster got me to calm down. "Come back over here and sit down," he said to me as he led me to the sofa.

The other agents that were in the other park of the house came to see what the commotion was all about. And once Agent Foster assured them that everything was under control, they went back to their posts.

I sat there on the chair and wondered if I'd ever leave this place alive. With the Carter brothers only a few miles away and Bishop in a fucking beach house plotting his next hit, I felt like a sitting duck.

DIAMOND AND HER ANTICS

"Bitch, why don't you just lay down and die?" Diamond asked. She seemed a bit frustrated. "What is it now?" I asked her. She stood before me with her hair and clothes in disarray. I knew she was dead, but she hadn't looked like she was withering away until now. The skin on her body looked like it was peeling away. I could literally see the skeletal bones in her hands and face. Death was becoming visible.

"You were supposed to die at the precinct."

"No shit! Everyone around me was firing their fucking guns over my head." I commented.

"So, why won't you just lay down and die?" Diamond pressed the issue.

"Because I wanna live. Do you think I wanna end up like you?"

"It's too late. You're running around on borrowed time."

"What do you want with me Diamond? Why do you keep appearing in my dreams?"

"Because this is the only time I can talk to you."

"What's the use? I'm not trying to hear anything you gotta say."

Diamond laughed. "I bet you'll listen to me if I tell you who's gonna take your life."

Diamond was right. Finding out who'd make an attempt on my life sparked my interest. I figured if she'd tell me, I'd be in a better position to stop them. So I called her bluff. "Tell me who's trying to kill me."

"Why should I do that?"

"Diamond, stop playing fucking games with me. You're gonna either tell me or you're not."

"Just know that I want you to experience the same fate I did. My death came unexpected and it was brutal. And if I spare you all of the trauma I had, it wouldn't be fun to watch when the day comes."

"I'm not listening to you anymore. You're a fucking train wreck!" I spat and then I turned to walk away from her. If I stood there and continued to entertain her bullshit, I'd look like a damn fool. Besides, she's delirious. And if she really knew when I was going to die then it wouldn't matter if I knew who was going to do it. When it's your time to go, then it's the end.

Right before I got out of Diamond's sight, she said something that stopped me in my tracks. "Agent Foster doesn't like you like you think." She said.

I instantly became offended by her comment. She doesn't know shit about Agent Foster. He and I had a special connection. And nothing she says will make me feel any different.

"So, what are you gonna tell me now? That he's the killer?"

"He might be. And I will say that he's using the hell out of you. And as soon as he gets you to testify against Bishop, he's gonna throw you to the wolves."

"Shut the fuck up! You don't know what you're talking about." I snapped.

"I know that he's gonna pass your dumb ass on to Detective Rosenberg and Whitfield once his investigation is over."

"He would never do that to me. And besides, how can they take me into custody when I haven't been charged with anything?"

"They're trumping up charges on your ass right now as we speak. But too bad, you're gonna be dead before they take you to trial." Diamond uttered and then she smiled.

"You think this shit is funny don't you?"

"It's gonna be even funnier when you cross over into my world."

"Diamond, I'm not coming down here with you so you can get that shit out of your head." I screamed. I screamed as loud as I possibly could so that I'd wake up. And guess what? It worked.

I laid in the bed and wondered if what Diamond told me about Agent Foster was true. It would devastate me if I found out what she said was true. So, how do I deal with it? And where do I go from here?

BLINDSIDED

After the dream I had last night with Diamond concerning Agent Foster, I started looking at him just like I looked at the other agents. Everybody around me became a suspect. My life was at stake and anyone of these sell-out motherfuckers could take it from me. Every one of them had their own personal firearms, and I didn't have shit. So, I was fair game all the way around the board.

Down in the kitchen area, Agent Foster, Zachary and Humphrey were all playing a game of poker. I stood at the doorway and watched them as they goofed around. The only person missing out of this bunch was Agent Rome. I didn't see him on my way down stairs so that made me wonder where he could be. I stepped away from the entryway of the kitchen and walked around to every room on the first floor and he was still nowhere in sight. "Seen Agent Rome?" I asked one of the agents standing guard in one of the rooms. "Not since about an hour ago." He said.

"A'ight thanks," I said and kept moving.

I looked in the bathroom on the first floor and when I saw that it was empty, I made my way back onto the second floor. Agent Rome had to be around somewhere. What he was doing, I had no clue but I was going to find out.

I searched around in the two bedrooms that were on the second floor but Agent Rome was still nowhere to be found. Once I searched every room on the second floor, I headed towards the bathroom because I heard whispering. I knew it was Agent Rome's voice but I couldn't make out what he was saying. The first thing that came to mind was that he was talking to someone on the phone and that peeked my interest. I thought to myself, why was he away from everyone talking in secret? Did he have something to hide? I tiptoed very quickly as I walked towards the bathroom and the closer I got the louder the whispering got. I started to get close enough to the door so I could eavesdrop on Agent Rome but when I heard him moan and say, "Ahhhh yeah," I became paralyzed. And quickly made the assumption that he was beating his dick while having phone sex. I guessed with all the time he spent watching over my life as well as his fellow agents; he needed to relieve some tension. I chuckled to myself and turned to go back to the first floor. I made it all the way to the staircase and was caught by surprise when the bathroom door opened. I turned around and saw Agent Rome accompanied by one of the other agents exiting the bathroom. My heart stopped at that moment. I couldn't believe my eyes when I witnessed Agent Rome zip up his pants while the other agent wiped his mouth with the back of his shirt sleeve. When they saw me, they looked like they saw a ghost. This was definitely an awkward moment for all of us. Realizing that Agent Rome wasn't on the phone and that he was actually getting his dick sucked by the other agent was a hard pill for me to swallow. I had no idea whether I should say something to them or just turn my head and keep it moving. They were grown ass men. So, who was I to judge them? But then I figured since I'd caught them in a very compromising position I held the cards to fuck their lives up any way I saw fit. And they knew it too.

"Are you okay?" Agent Rome asked me. His facial expression was cheesy looking. So I knew he was feeling me out.

"Oh yeah, I'm fine." I told him and then I took one foot forward to go back down the staircase.

The other agent turned his head as if I had just reprimanded him. But I saw through his actions, he knew I knew about their little liaison. To put it in layman terms, I knew he'd just blown Agent Rome's dick. I started to tell him to turn his ass around and get a toothbrush to his mouth, but I knew that it would've been inappropriate so I left well enough alone and made my way down stairs.

I'M IN ANOTHER WORLD

Back in the kitchen Agent Foster and the other agents were still playing their game of poker when I crossed the entryway. My facial expression must've given away my sudden mood change because Agent Foster looked at me and said, "What's wrong with you?" I tried with every fiber of my body to act like I was fine but somehow I missed the mark. He didn't believe me when I told him there wasn't anything wrong with me. "Are you sure?" he continued to question me.

I gave him a half smile. "Yes, I'm sure." And then I felt a cool draft pass me. I looked behind me and saw Agent Rome had entered into the kitchen as well. His dick sucking agent lover didn't join us. He probably thought I was going to blow the whistle on their asses. But I wasn't going to utter one word. If they want to blow each other off then that's their business. I'm just gonna stay out of their way. My main priority is myself. Nobody else.

"Where you been Rome? I've been in here kicking ass and taking names." Agent Foster said in a jokingly manner.

Agent Rome went straight to the refrigerator and grabbed himself a cold can of Pepsi. He flicked back the metal opener and put the can up to his mouth. He swallowed half the soda in ten seconds flat. He let out a loud burp when he was done. "Excuse me." He said.

I looked at him with as much disgust I could muster up. The other agents witnessed it. But Agent Zachary was the only one who made mentioned of it. "You're looking at Rome like you despise him." She commented. I knew she was trying to put me on blast but I didn't feed into her bullshit. She was a messy ass bitch.

I looked at Agent Zachary with the same expression I gave Agent Rome. I wanted her to know that I wasn't in the mood for her shit. Not today.

"Shit, you sure you okay," Agent Foster asked me. By this time, all eyes were on me. The card game had actually come to a halt. I didn't want this attention. The irony of it all was that Agent Rome ended up leaving out of the kitchen. "Lynise, is everything good," Agent Foster asked again. "Rome, get your ass back in here."

Shit, this was not what I wanted. I didn't want us to be in a confrontation. I had been told that I wear my emotions on my shoulders too much and this was definitely one of those times.

As soon Agent Rome came back in the kitchen, Agent Foster asked, "What in the hell is going on between you and Lynise?"

Agent Rome looked at me. I was surprised, you couldn't tell anything by the look on his face. "I must apologize to Ms. Carter, Sir. I tried to make conversation with her upstairs and she didn't want to talk to me, so I said some choice words. So, Lynise, I'm sorry for my actions."

This motherfucker was really taking a chance that I would go along with his lame ass excuse. Although his expression wasn't showing it, I could tell he was really hoping I would co-sign his bullshit ass lie. And after careful consideration, I decided to do just that. Yes, I let his dumb ass slip through the cracks. But little did he know that I was going to tax his ass later. He was going to pay dearly before it was all over.

"No problem," I said weakly. "I shouldn't have just walked off when you were trying to talk to me."

"People, I understand all the shit we are going through and the tension that is increasing on a daily basis," Agent Foster began. "But we have to stick together. And I think it's better if we try to get along versus disliking each other. Fuck, dislike the situation. Shit, we all do. But dislike the motherfucker who have us in this predicament—that motherfucker Bishop."

"Amen to that," Agent Rome said. He sounded like a fake ass preacher. I wanted to throw his ass some shade but I left well enough alone. I knew I'd have my time with him. And that time couldn't come soon enough.

Agent Rome finally left the kitchen and I was on his heel. He walked past the living room and took the stairs two at a time as he made his way upstairs. I was still on his coattail though. And when he got to the top, he suddenly stopped and I actually ran into his ass.

"What, Lynise? What do you want from me?" he said in a low voice.

I walked past him and went into the first bedroom I came to and turned around. He was looking at me and I gave him a look that said, "Get your ass in here."

As soon as he walked across the threshold, I jumped his shit. "I like that stunt you pulled on me downstairs."

"What else was I supposed to say?" he whispered.

"If you were bold enough to let another man suck on your dick then you should be bold enough to let the world know." I replied sarcastically. I had to let him know that I wasn't some gullible ass chick running around here with my head stuck up my ass. I knew what time it was. So, he should too.

"It's so much more complicated than you think." He said.

"Didn't I hear you say that you had a wife at home?" I questioned him. I needed to give him a reality check.

"Come on Lynise, that's a low blow! Leave my wife out of this." He snapped. He didn't raise her voice though. He kept his volume down to a minimum.

"So what am I supposed to do? Walk around here like nothing happened?"

"That's about the sum of it." He said with a stern face.

"Listen Agent Rome, I don't want to come off like I'm blackmailing you or anything. But, if you want me to keep your business on the hush-hush, you're gonna have to do something for me."

Agent Rome acted like he wasn't too pleased with my proposal. But he got over his feelings very quickly. "What do you want?" he finally asked me after he looked over his shoulders to see if anyone was around.

"I want you to help me get away from here. It's really not safe for me to be around here. You saw all those people trying to kill me. I even got Bishop trying to take me out. So, the sooner I get out of here, the better off everyone will be."

"I don't know Lynise." Agent Rome responded in a way as if he was in deep thought. Then he looked over his shoulder once more.

"Look, all you gotta do is let me walk out the front door and I will never look back." I told him.

"How am I going to do that when there's a ton of agents patrolling this house?" he continued to explain in a low like whisper.

"Get your boyfriend to help. Maybe he could distract the other agents while I slip away."

"What if we get caught?"

"We won't if you do what you're supposed to do."

Agent Rome turned and looked over his shoulders again. Then he turned his attention back towards me. "I'll tell you what, let me speak with Agent Mann and I'll get back with you in the morning."

"You do that." I told him.

IT'S TIME TO GO

After having a chat with Agent Rome I closed the door to my room and laid down on the bed. I had to devise a plan to get out of here. And even though Agent Rome hadn't given me the go ahead, I knew how much power I had over him so there was no doubt in my mind that he would come on board. Now all I had to do was think about the best way to escape.

While I was in deep thought I heard a lot of moving around outside in the hallway. I didn't know who it was until I heard Agent Foster's voice. "Stop it," he said. His voice was barely audible.

"Come on, you know you want me." I heard her say. Her voice was seductive. Unfortunately, it didn't do her any good.

"Stop before someone hears you," Agent Foster warned her. He tried his best to whisper but it didn't work.

Without hesitation I eased off the bed and tiptoed over to the bedroom door. I had to see what was going on. "Why are you pushing me away? You fucked me the other night with no problems." Agent Zachary spat. I could tell she was furious. And she wanted the entire house to know that too.

"Shhhh..." I heard Agent Foster say.

"Don't shhh...me! Whatcha don't want your informant to hear us?" she barked.

I turned the doorknob very slowly and pulled the door opened but I couldn't see anything. Agent Foster or Agent Zachary were nowhere in sight. I started to peek my head around the corner of the doorway but I didn't want to get caught eavesdropping.

"I'm not dealing with this shit right now. I'm going downstairs," he snapped and then I heard him march down the stairs.

"Well fuck it then!" she spat.

I stood still not knowing whether to open the door further or shut it altogether. I wanted to see Agent Zachary badly. Seeing her face after Agent Foster had just dissed her would be totally satisfying. She had been a thorn in my side since day one. Besides that, she had just called me a fucking informant. How fucked up was that? I mean who the fuck does she think she is? Informant or not, I was once a chick bartending at a local strip club so that I could pay my bills. And then life happened. So, she can stop riding my ass and get a life of her own.

After a little bit of thought I decided to close the bedroom door. I pushed it slowly in the opposite direction but things never go as planned. Startled by an unexpected blow to the door, I jumped back and that's when I noticed that Agent Zachary had forced the bedroom door back with her left foot. "Did you get an earful?" she frowned at me.

"I heard enough." I replied sarcastically.

Agent Zachary probably thought I was going to back down from her considering she was an agent and all. But I had to let her know that I wasn't afraid of her. I was from the streets. And the only thing I was afraid of was a loaded gun to my head. Nothing else.

Not pleased with my response, Agent Zachary pushed the bedroom door completely open and then she stepped inside the room. She took five steps total. And was only about two feet away from me. "So, you heard me when I called you an informant, huh?"

"Yeah, I heard that. And I heard when Agent Foster told you that he didn't have time for your shit. Sounds like there's trouble in paradise to me." I smiled.

"Bitch, you can smile all you want. But you'll never end up with him. He's a government agent. And government personnel never run off into the sunset with criminals. So, just know that that little ten minute fuck fest you two had was just that, a fuck fest. He will never wife you up. You're beneath him. So, stay in your lane." She said and then she turned around and left.

I started to run behind her and curse her ass out but I left her alone. I figured why waste my time? I was on some different shit. I was trying to get out of here without her or Agent Foster's knowledge. My whole objective was to leave this fucking dump and never run into any of these assholes again. And if that meant being on the run for the rest of my life, then so be it.

THE DEAL OF A LIFETIME

I stayed clear of Agent Zachary's dumb ass after that run in she and I had the night before. I was focused on meeting back up with Agent Rome so we could discuss my escape plan. Like every morning, everyone met down in the kitchen area to break bread and eat breakfast together. Good thing, this wasn't Agent Rome's morning to cook. So, while everyone else was standing around eating and making small talk, I arranged for Agent Rome and I to meet back inside my bedroom.

He was eight minutes late, and I made sure he knew it. "Why are you so late? Whatcha' trying to do, get us railroaded?" I barked. I felt like he needed to know that my time was sensitive and that we needed to stay on course.

Agent Rome looked over his shoulders to make sure the coast was clear and then he closed the bedroom door behind himself.

"I had to make sure everybody was downstairs before I came up here." He whispered.

"Just tell me are you in or out?" I got straight to the point. I didn't want to hear anything else. My main focus was to come up with a getaway plan. That was it.

"Agent Mann said he'd help. But it's gonna have to go down tonight."

"Why tonight? That's not giving us enough time to plan." I griped.

"Because he's getting pulled from this detail in the morning. He was told by our head office that he and one of the other agents gotta' head back to New Jersey. That incident that happened with our supervisor Joyce is calling for a bunch of our agents to go in the field." He explained.

"Tonight," I said, trying to register the word in my mind. I was taken aback by the mere thought of the urgency that has to take place if I wanted to get out of here.

"Yes, you're gonna have to leave here tonight."

One part of me wanted to be overjoyed because I wanted nothing else but to leave this mad house. I figured my life would be safer if I got away from these incompetent ass FBI agents. But the other part of me got this sudden feeling of anxiety. The awful feeling of not knowing what would be around the corner after I left this place was scary. My stomach was literally turning into knots. "So, what's the plan?" I asked him. It felt like my words were going in slow motion.

"You're gonna have to leave after midnight which is when all the agents switch posts. Agent Mann and I figured that if you act like you gotta' use the bathroom or wandered off to the kitchen for a late night snack, you'll be able to slip out the back door with no problems. Remember when we switch posts they'll be a minute and a half window of opportunity for you to run away from the house. None of the agents will be watching the perimeter during that time."

"What about the windows and door alarms? You know they chime every time someone opens them."

"Yes, they do. But, I'll deactivate the system long enough for you to slip away."

"Well, what are you going to tell Agent Foster when he finds out that I'm gone?"

"You don't need to worry about that. Just be ready to go when we give you the cue."

"Will I be able to take any of my things?" I had to ask.

"It'll be too risky if you do."

"What about my purse? I'm gonna need that."

"You can take it just as long as you hide underneath your clothing."

"Think this is going to work?"

"If everything goes according to plan. Yes."

I took a deep breath and then I exhaled. "All right, well let's do it." I finally said.

I watched Agent Rome as he exited my room. And when he closed the door behind himself, I laid down on my bed and thought about where I was going to go the moment I stepped foot outside. The sound of freedom was near.

MINDING MY BUSINESS

Agent Foster was chilling down stairs in the living room area when I laid my eyes on him. Agent Zachary sat across from him in another chair. Agent Rome was also in attendance. So Agent Mann was standing alongside of him. I couldn't help but look at the clock on the wall. It was twelve noon, which meant I had twelve hours before I would be free to go off and do what the fuck I wanted to do. I would be free from seeing Bishop. Free from being around the FEDS. And I'd be free and far away from the Carter brothers. I didn't need Witness Protection because I wasn't going to testify against anyone including Bishop. That wasn't my case. That was his case. And as far as Duke Carrington's case, that wasn't my case either. Every bad thing Duke and Diamond threw into the atmosphere came tumbling back towards them. My battle was over. And so was my stint in this place.

"Why are you looking at the clock? Got somewhere to be?" Agent Foster blurted out.

Fear stricken, I looked straight at Agent Rome. My first thought was had he told Agent Foster our plans? I searched his face and he looked as shocked as I was. "Why are you looking at Agent Rome? He can't help you." Agent Foster joked. He must've thought he was being amusing. Agent Zachary must've felt he was amusing too because she cracked a smile.

I knew I couldn't lose my cool. Giving Agent Foster the slightest inclination that I was up to no good would've been a dead giveaway. So, I came back strong and said, "Have I ever looked at Agent Rome for help in the past?"

"That's what I know." Agent Rome continued to laugh.

"Well, there you go." I said and walked towards the kitchen.

"You still haven't told us where you were going?" Agent Foster pressed the issue.

My heart was pounding uncontrollably. I didn't know whether to throw my hands up and give up or stand my ground. Luckily Agent Rome came to my defense, "Y'all leave her alone because I'm truly not in the mood to hear her mouth." He blurted out.

I thought it was genius of him to come to my rescue the way that he did. Everyone in the room knew he and I didn't get along so it would've looked somewhat suspicious if he had jumped to my defense. So, to act like he didn't want to hear my mouth was brilliant.

"Yes, please listen to him before I start running my mouth and saying shit y'all ain't gonna want to hear." I commented.

A minute later Agent Foster got up from the chair and followed me into the kitchen. I saw him coming towards me through my peripheral vision. I also saw Agent Zachary gritting on me from the sideline. I knew she was boiling on the inside.

"Let me holler at you for a moment." Agent Foster said.

I turned around towards him and said, "Go ahead, talk." I insisted.

"Sit down." He instructed me as he pulled a chair out from the table.

I took a seat in the chair he pulled from the table. And then I watched him as he sat down in the chair across from me. As much as I wanted to act calm, the nervous chick on the inside of me was trying to come out. Agent Foster had this way about him that intimidated the hell out of me. "What's up?" I said, not knowing how he was going to respond.

"I got a call from those two homicide detectives early this morning and they're saying that they need to see you again. But I told them that wasn't gonna happen right now because you're under federal protection for another case."

"And what about that shit that went down at the precinct when we were there? I almost got killed. So, do they expect me to let that shit happen again?"

"They know we're not gonna risk putting you in harms way again. So they're saying that they're willing to meet us on our terms."

"But why? I told them everything I knew. There's nothing else to talk about." I replied. I was getting irritated by the second. I didn't want to see those idiots again. I wanted to be left alone."

"Tell me something,"

"Yeah, what is it?"

"Tell me about Duke Carrington and the Carter brothers. Tell me why those detectives are hounding you for more information concerning those guys?

"I don't know." I said. I tried to give Agent Foster the sincerest expression I could muster up.

"What's this I hear about an illegal adoption agency? I heard he and another guy were involved in over two dozen murders."

I hesitated for a moment to think about what I was going to say. I knew I had to take my time and say the right words to prevent from incriminating myself. Agent Foster was a very smart man. He saw bullshit from a mile away. So, I knew I needed to be on my "A" game.

"Duke was taking babies from young girls and killing the girls afterwards and selling the babies to rich families," I blurted out all at once.

"Wow! He was the one the killing girls?"

"Yeah,"

"What about the doctor? What role did he play?"

"He was the one performing the deliveries. He had a hand in killing some of the girls too." I answered his question.

While I continued to tell Agent Foster my version of the tale involving Duke Carrington, Agent Rome walked in the kitchen and interrupted us. "Foster we got two black SUV's with tinted windows parked outside the house."

"What's the problem?" Agent Foster asked.

"The problem is, those SUV's have been sitting out there for over thirty minutes and no one has gotten in it or out of it since it arrived."

Agent Foster looked at Agent Rome in a peculiar way. Then he stood to his feet. "Go check the perimeter." He instructed him. Agent Zachary and Mann go with him."

I stood to my feet. I wasn't going to be a sitting duck this time around. I was not about to let another person roll up on me without warning. I'm walking out of here on my two feet, not a body bag.

After I got up from the chair, I watched Agent Foster pull out his weapons and put on his flak vest. "Go into your room until I tell you otherwise." He instructed me. Once again I was on high alert running around like my mind was going bad. What kind of life was this? I shouldn't have to run around in fear every minute of the day. Who does that?

On my way back to my room I watched as the agents scrambled to their posts. "Is everyone in position?" I heard Agent Foster yell over his radio.

"Yes," everyone spoke into unison.

"Does everyone have a visual?" Agent Foster's questions continued.

"Yes," I heard Agent Rome say.

"Yes, I'm good on this end," Agent Zachary said.

"What about you Mann and Humphreys?" Agent Forster asked.

"Yeah, we're good too," Agent Mann replied.

I sat on the floor of the closet in my bedroom. I sat in a squat position with my head pressed against my knees. My heart continued to race as I contemplated the outcome of this ordeal. I didn't know if I was going to come out of this thing injured or even dead for that matter. It just seemed like everyday I'm thrown into another distressed situation. "Has anyone seen any movement yet?" I heard Agent Foster yell over the radio.

"No, I'm not getting any action over here." Agent Zachary replied.

"Yeah, Foster, I'm not getting anything either." Agent Rome said over the radio.

"It's dead over here too," I head Agent Mann said.

"Well, what in the hell are they doing? Agent Foster asked.

"I think a couple of us need to go out there and see what's going on." Agent Humphrey's said.

"Yeah, I think so." I heard Agent Zachary say over the radio.

"Agent Rome, you and Mann take Agent Humphreys outside and find out what's going on, Agent Foster instructed them.

"Roger that," Agent Rome said.

"Stay online so I can hear you." Agent Foster instructed.

"Got it," Agent Rome replied and then the communication stopped.

I heard the agents that Agent Foster summoned to go outside ran pass my room. It sounded like a real live stampede. All sorts of thoughts came to mind while I sat there in the closet. My first thought was that now would be a good time to make a run for it considering everyone's attention had been diverted to those two SUVs outside. But then I thought, what if I fucked up and got caught trying to get away and then I mess up my other chance of leaving tonight? I'd be devastated if I fucked up my chance of leaving this God forsaken place. So, I figured it would be smart of me to chill out and let this whole thing play out. But if those niggas down in those trucks were sent by the Carter brothers, then all bets are off. I'm bailing out of here, with or without Agent Rome and Mann's help.

What Doesn't Kill Us, Makes Us Crazy

It seemed like I had been sitting in this closet forever. I couldn't hear or see anything and that had become a problem. I mean what if something happen? I wouldn't be prepared if this house came under attack. I'd be in some serious trouble. So, I figured the best thing for me to do was to check things out on my own.

On my way out of the closet I heard Agent Foster's voice sound over the radio. "What's going on out there?"

"We're approaching the vehicles now." Agent Rome radioed back.

I jumped to my feet. I was curious to see what was about to go down. So I sprinted over to the window and then I adjusted the mini blinds in a way that I could see out of the window but someone on the outside wouldn't be able to see me.

My heart skipped a beat when I saw Agent Rome, Mann and Humphreys as they approached the parked SUVs from behind. They had their guns drawn and they had them aimed directly at the windows of those vehicles.

They were acting like they were SWAT. I could tell that those men were highly trained. "Open the doors slowly and get out with your hands in the air." I heard both Agent Rome and Humphreys yell. Agent Rome and Agent Mann were both posted up by the first truck while Agent Humphreys stood by the second truck.

Three seconds passed and the doors to both SUVs opened up. I saw hands raised in the air as the people emerged from the trucks. I saw a total of ten hands raised high and when the men stepped from behind the doors dressed in plain clothes Agent Rome and Mann started yelling at them. I got a good look at the Caucasian men after they stepped out of the vehicles. There was so much chaos outside Agent Foster instructed another one of the agents to accompany Agent Rome and the others. "These men are saying they're narcotics detectives." I heard Agent Rome yell over the radio.

"Get their badges." Agent Foster told Agent Rome.

"I'm doing that right now." Agent Rome replied.

Within minutes every one of the Caucasian men dressed in regular civilian clothes were identified. I overheard Agent Rome when he confirmed that those men were in deed undercover narcotics detectives staking out a known marijuana stash house that was a half block up the street. I'm sure it was a bittersweet feeling for all the agents.

But who would've thought that there was a weed spot a half block down the street from a federal hideout? Those cats had set up a smoke spot right underneath our noses. How clever was that? Thanks to New Jersey's Finest now the local narcotic detectives investigation had been compromised because of all the commotion that was caused. What's even worse was that the detectives had to start their investigation over from scratch. What a waste of time?

After things were settled between the agents and the narcotic detectives all the agents returned back to the house. Agent Foster sat down in the living room area and briefed everyone in the house. I stayed upstairs. I used this time to go over my escape plan. Agent Rome told me tonight had to be the night so I conditioned my mind on how I was going to maneuver through the streets of Newport News once I was free. Newport News was a tough place. And they had some dangerous people roaming the streets. But I convinced myself that I shouldn't worry about that. This was my chance to leave and I was taking it. And even though we'd just had a false alarm, I refused to go through another episode of ducking and dodging bullets. I wasn't built for this type of shit. Nor was I in the right frame of mind for it. I just wanted to live a normal life for once. Was that too much to ask for?

MORE & MORE LIES

Time was winding down and I only had one hour left before I was a free woman. Agent Rome and I went over the plan again about fifteen minutes ago so we should be rock solid when the time came. Agent Foster checked on me a couple of times through out the day. He wanted to know why I'd been so shut off from everyone. I gave him this bogus ass excuse about how it was that time of the month for me. "When my cycle comes on, I come down with these awful cramps and I get bloated. And to keep from snapping at somebody I just decided to keep to myself." I told him.

He told me he understand and finally left me alone. After Agent Foster left my room Agent Zachary reared her ugly ass face. She tried to act like she was just randomly walking by, but I peeped her move. I'm a woman. And I knew the type of games women played. I swear I wished I could tell her that after tonight she didn't have to worry about me. I was going to be out of her hair once and for all. I might just leave the dumb bitch a note telling her how stupid she was. Dumb bitches are everyway!

When I realized that I had five minutes left before the big moment, my heart started doing somersaults and I became full of anxiety. I was literally getting cold feet so I was tempted to tell Agent Rome that I wasn't going to leave. It was dark as hell outside and I wasn't sure if I was ready to go out there by myself. But something inside of me convinced me that I would be all right and all I had to do was take the opportunity given to me.

"Are you ready?" Agent Mann asked me when he approached the entryway of my bedroom door.

My heart was pounding rapidly. "Yeah, I'm ready." I told him. I stood there before him fully clothe with my purse tucked away underneath my shirt.

"Well, go downstairs to the kitchen and wait in the food pantry until I give you the word to run." He instructed me.

"Where is Agent Rome?" I whispered.

"He's making his rounds and then he's going to deactivate the alarm system."

"Where is Agent Foster?" my questions continued. I was nervous and the only thing that would make me feel a little more assured was to find out where everyone was.

"He's in the bathroom."

"What about Agent Zachary?"

"I'm not sure. She's probably on her way to her new post. So, you better get downstairs right now."

Feeling the urgency in his voice I followed his instructions and headed down to the kitchen. By the time I made it to the bottom stair Agent Foster walked out of the bathroom just before I turned the corner. "Hey where you going?" He yelled in a jokingly manner.

I stopped in my tracks. My body was consumed with fear but I didn't let that distract me from the goal ahead. "I'm going to get some water. I'll be right back." I told him and then I proceeded towards he kitchen.

I thank God no one was in the kitchen. It was totally empty. So without hesitation I went into the food pantry and closed the door behind myself. But as soon as I entered into the pantry I was coming out of it. Agent Mann opened the door one minute later. "Come on let's go." He told me.

I followed Agent Mann out of the food pantry and allowed him to lead me towards the back door. He grabbed the doorknob and turned it very slow. And immediately after he pulled the door open, he looked at me and said, "Go now," and pushed me outside. I didn't have time to look back at him because as soon as my feet touched the ground Agent Mann closed the back door. It happened so quickly. The fresh air hit me like a ton of bricks and it felt good. But I wanted more so I put one foot in front of the other and ran away from the house as fast as I could. There was a fence that separated the backyard from the other houses around it. It wasn't that tall and if I wanted to climb cross it all I had to do was flip my body over it and I'd be home free.

Before I hopped over the fence I heard a voice say, "Hey," and when I turned around to see what it was, I was struck with a blow to the head. BOOM! I fell to the ground. I looked up but my vision was blurry. I wanted desperately to see who had just hit me and when my eyes finally adjusted there was Agent Rome standing right before me with his pistol pointed directly at me. "Did you really think I was going to let you go just like that?" he asked me.

I laid there on my back not knowing whether to scream for help or plead for my life. But it became clear that if I screamed I'd be dead before Agent Foster or anyone else for that matter would be able to save me. I was in this situation alone and I had to deal with it. "Please don't kill me." I begged him.

"It's too late for that bitch. You're dying tonight." He growled. His voice was intimating. And I sensed that he was serious. But I couldn't give up that easy. I figured if I stalled him long enough Agent Foster would realized that I had slipped away and come to my rescue.

"Agent Rome if you let me live I promise I won't tell anyone about you and Agent Mann. It'll be our secret. I give you my word." I cried out.

"Fuck your word! I'm ending this shit now." He said and as soon as he pulled back on the chamber he pointed his pistol at me. I closed my eyes.

"Agent Rome is that you out there?" I heard Agent Foster yell from the house.

I immediately opened my eyes and noticed that Agent Rome had turned his attention towards the house. He and I both saw Agent Foster standing at the back door to the house. The light in the kitchen was on and he stood in the middle of it. I could see him just as clear as day. And just for a brief moment I saw hope. "Agent Rome's trying to kill me!" I yelled.

Startled by my sudden outburst, Agent Rome turned back towards me. But by this time I was up on my feet. And my first thought was to knock the gun from his hands and that's just what I did. "You stupid bitch!" he snapped after the gun fell from his hand. He went into panic mode because he had lost control of this situation. And he knew he'd only be able to regain control if he got his weapon back in his hand. So he scrambled around on the ground in search of his gun.

From that moment I saw a small window of opportunity so I took it. I heard Agent Foster behind me calling my name but I ignored him. I had to go now. So, I grabbed ahold of the fence and flipped my entire body of it. I lost my step and and hit the ground on the other side hard. Pain shot through my body going one hundred miles an hour. But that didn't stop me. I got up on my feet and ran as fast as I could. The streets were dark but it didn't matter to me. I knew that I had to get out of there. I heard Agent Foster calling my name behind me but I refused to look back. I was on a mission. And so far, I was on the right path. To hell with Agent Foster and the rest of the agents. To hell with Bishop and the Carter brothers too. Aside from my purse, I didn't have anything but the clothes on my back. But in the end I knew I was going to be okay, especially if I went somewhere were no one knew me. Maybe then I'd be able to start my life over.

FREEDOM

I knew I had walked at least two miles before my feet started feeling it, which was why I flagged down a cab. I was on Jefferson Avenue walking by a gas station when I saw a cab driver pumping gas into his car. I approached him and asked him if he'd give me a lift. "You got money?" he asked me.

"Yeah, I got money." I assured him.

He was a black man. He was a short and stocky guy. And when he opened his mouth I could tell that he was a true gentleman. "Where are you going?" he asked me after he started up the engine.

I hesitated for a second and then I said, "Can you take me to Norfolk?"

"That's going to be a seventy-five dollar fare."

"Okay. That's no problem. I got it."

"Well, I'm going to need you to pay me now. And whatever is left I will refund you."

"Here you go." I told him after I grabbed money from my purse.

After he took the money from my hand he sped off and jumped on the nearest highway. "What part of Norfolk am I taking you to?

"I'm not sure. But I'll let you know as soon as we come out of the Hampton Bridge Tunnel." I replied.

"Am I bringing you back to Newport News?" he wondered aloud.

"No. You're dropping me off."

"You must be going over your boyfriend's house, huh?" I could tell he wanted to make small talk.

"No, I'm going over my best friend's house." I lied. I mean was I supposed to tell him that I had just escaped from a safe house that was heavily guarded by FBI agents? Hell no!

"Why are you out this time of the night?"

"I was waiting on my ride to pick me up but they never came." I continued to lie. I couldn't let him in on the truth. I'd compromise my freedom if I did.

"Well, whoever stood you up was a damn fool."

"Tell me about it." I commented. I gave him a half smile.

The cab driver ended up talking my head off during the course of the drive to Norfolk. And as soon as we crossed over the bridge and traveled through the Hampton Bridge Tunnel, the cab driver took the first exit, which was the Willoughby Spit exit. "Why are we taking this exit?" I inquired.

The cab driver looked back at me through the rearview mirror and said, "Shut up bitch! You're about to go on the ride of your life."

Fear stricken all over again, I managed to cry out, "Oh my God! You're that serial killer that's been killing all those women."

SNEAK PEEK INTO THE "NEW YORK'S FINEST SERIES"

When I first laid eyes on the Federal Agents who were being accompanied by the airport police, I damn near had a heart attack. They were fifty feet away from me. If I wanted to make my escape, then now was the perfect time. Unfortunately for me, every government agent with a badge and gun had every exit in this entire fucking airport blocked off. So the possibilities of me getting away from law enforcement were *slim to improbable*. And even if they weren't, where would I go?

Immediately after I got word that our entire operation blew up in our faces, we got word that the Feds were about to make their arrests, so I was given instructions to go to my place to clean out my safe, erase my hard-drive on my laptop and get my ass over to the hideaway apartment Reggie and I had across town. It was a place no one knew about but the three of us.

Meanwhile the Feds and the airport police were minutes from closing in on me. I tried to figure out my next step as my heart raced uncontrollably. The edge I had over them was that they were looking for a young woman fitting my description and not a senior citizen woman wearing a grayish colored wig with streaks of black, an old faded blue dress, a pair of orthopedic shoes and walked with a cane. Believe me, I acted the part on queue and used my knowledge of the airport's security system to my advantage. Only a select few of the employees knew the airport was equipped with over a thousand rotating surveillance cameras and fortunately for me, I was one of them. I also knew there were so many cameras that the security staff could not observe them all simultaneously, which immediately prompted me to change my escape plan.

The airport's generator room was only three feet from me. I eased towards the door very carefully. I acted as if I had lost something on the floor and right before I swiped my key card to make my entry, I glanced around the concourse to make sure I was free and clear. When I realized passengers and airline staff had fixed their attention on the manpower search that had engulfed the entire airport, I knew now was the perfect time to make my exit.

Without hesitation, I swiped my key card and pushed the door open. And just when I thought I was about to make a clean getaway, the security alarm went off. Immediately, my body became panic stricken. I didn't know whether to proceed through the door or turn back around. But as soon as I heard several of the law enforcement officers yell from behind me, I instantly looked back and noticed a horde of law enforcement types rapidly rushing towards me. I could tell by the expressions on their faces that they wanted me badly. I slammed the door shut and looked around the machine-filled room for something I could use to barricade the door. My heart beat at an incredible pace as I scanned and moved around the room. Then I finally saw a pipe lying next to one of the big generators. I snatched it up from the floor and said a quiet and quick prayer as I raced back to the door. I heard the commotion on the other side of the door. There were at least two different voices yelling obscenities as they struggled to get the door open.

"Who has a fucking key card?" I heard one officer yell over top of the loud blaring sound of the security alarm.

That question alone gave me a glimmer of hope that I may be able to prevent them from getting into this room. Now I had to hurry and place the pipe between the crease of the metal bar and the floor. So when they tried to push the door open, the pipe wouldn't allow the door to move one inch.

Not even ten seconds after I placed the pipe against the door, I heard a loud booming sound hit the door. BOOM! But the door didn't budge. "On the count of three, let's hit it again," I heard one of the officers yell. On the count of three, I watched nervously as they hit the door again. But the door didn't budge. "She's gotta have something barricading the door," I heard another male's voice yell over the top of the continued blaring sounds coming from the alarm system.

Knowing that they had figured out what I had done sent my mind into overdrive. I knew I had very limited time to find my way out of this room before they found a way inside. I had to get a move on it if I wanted to escape this madness.

When I turned around to bolt into the opposite direction, I was stopped in my tracks by a police-issued .40 caliber Glock.

"Where the fuck you think you're going?" said a man's voice as he pointed his pistol directly in my face.

The words *slim to improbable* reverberated throughout my mind as I looked down the biggest barrel I had ever been face-to-face with.

NEW YORK'S FINEST | KIKI SWINSON

CHAPTER 1

I was elated when the pilot finally landed our aircraft. We had been in the air for five and a half damn hours. The flights from San Diego to LaGuardia were always long and hard on my stomach. Having worked for the airlines for a little over five years, you would think I would be used to it by now. But unfortunately I wasn't.

What I had gotten used to were the perks of being a flight attendant. A lot of my co-workers weren't aware of it, but I was *New York's Finest.* I was a fly chick from Harlem and I was very popular amongst the men who were elite members of the airline and flew first class. I had them eating out of my fucking hands.

To get straight to the point, I'd befriended and fucked most of them. In return, they'd give me monetary gifts as well as expensive gold and diamond jewelry. Some would say I was being the typical flight attendant, fucking a passenger on every flight. But there was nothing atypical about what I was doing. I didn't consider myself a whore, but this pussy wasn't cheap; hence, the gold and diamond pussy. But the best connections I scored were three passengers who had lucrative drug connections. Unfortunately, after several deals, only one outlasted the other two. His name was Juan Alvarez.

Alvarez was from Costa Rica but he owned a lot of prime real estate here in New York. Not only did he have plenty of money, he had sex appeal. We dated for a few months. During that time I introduced him to my brother, Reggie. Alvarez and Reggie hit if off well and from there, we started a moneymaking enterprise that couldn't be tampered with. While I needed to make more money than the measly $17 an hour I was receiving from the airlines, Reggie needed a consistent supplier and Juan needed someone to put his coke on the streets. So it became a win-win situation for everyone involved.

Alvarez was a womanizer and when I learned that, I cut our relationship short. But we didn't end our business relationship. In the world we both grew up in, money talked and bullshit walked. Juan, Reggie and I had a good business venture, and more importantly, we had a means of transport—my flights to and fro locations across the globe. And as long as I had my bag handlers, TSA agents and mules help get Juan's coke through the airports, he promised he'd continue to supply Reggie and then we all would be happy.

After all the passengers exited our aircraft, my fellow flight attendants, Brooke and Kelsey, inspected the aisles and seats to ensure passengers hadn't left any of their belongings behind. Once that task was completed, we exited the plane ourselves.

I retrieved my Blackberry from my carry-on bag as I entered the airport and called Reggie. I had his number on speed dial, so it only took a matter of seconds to get him on the line.

"What's good?" he asked. He sounded very excited to hear from me. As a matter of fact, he'd always got excited when I called him after I came in from a flight. He knew that once he heard my voice, I had some high quality product coming his way.

"I hear the cheer in your voice," I told him.

"You damn right! When I hear your voice it makes me happy. Not only do I know that you're home safe, I also know that you've brought home some shit that's going to make us richer than we were yesterday."

I chuckled at Reggie's comment. He was a comedian in his own right. But he was better at selling coke. I introduced Juan to Reggie six months ago and since then, Reggie and I have generated a large sum of cash. I can't count Reggie's money, but I can say that I had saved over two million dollars. I thought about quitting my job as a flight attendant several times, but Reggie stressed over a dozen times how he needed someone on the inside to watch over his investments. He figured that if I left the airline, then he wouldn't have a set of trusting eyes watching to make sure his packages arrived safely into New York. So that's one of the reasons why I was still employed.

"Where are you?" I asked.

"I'm cross town at Malika's apartment. But I'm about to head back uptown because Vanessa's been ringing my Blackberry off the fucking hook. I told her I was out handling business but for some reason she doesn't believe me."

I chuckled once again. "Come on Reggie, are you listening to yourself? You've cheated on her over a dozen times since you two have been married, so ask yourself why should she believe you?"

He totally ignored my question. The only thing he wanted to talk about was how pure his coke was and how much money he stood to make. And immediately after I gave him the numbers we ended our conversation. Before we hung up, I assured him I would go to the TSA office to check up on the bags to make sure they hadn't been tampered with. And then I'd put them in the right hands, so he could get them before nightfall.

I had had a long day, but when I looked at how much I had accomplished, I felt good. Normally when I came home from a long flight, I'd take a hot shower and then I'd slip into my terrycloth pajamas and watch a couple of Blue Ray movies. Tonight, I decided to order Chinese and then hit the sack.

While I waited for my Chinese food to be delivered, I got a phone call from my sister-in-law, Vanessa. From time to time she'd pick up the phone to call me when she needed advice on how to handle certain situations with Reggie. I pretty much listened to her take on things, but at the end of the day my allegiance was with my brother. I would never sell him out even if he were wrong. He was my blood. And whether Vanessa realized it by now, Reggie was going to do what the fuck he wanted and when he wanted, and there's nothing she or I could do to change that.

Reggie has been and always will be a fucking street hustler. Our father was a street cat, so hustling ran through our blood strong. Reggie had stepped the game up big time. He excelled as an athlete in high school—the star running back on our football team and the point guard in basketball. Even then he was a hustler. He ran a betting racket on the football and basketball games he played in. Amazingly, as teenagers we were raking in bags of dough. As the dude setting the line, and the athlete controlling the results, we always won both on the field and in the streets. And it all computed to one thing—mo' money, mo' money. And that's some real shit!

"Naomi, you need to talk to your brother before I get his ass locked up!" she yelled. Her tone was sharp and I could tell that she was extremely angry. I could also tell that she was pacing the floor in their one million dollar home. She was known for rocking four and a half inch Giuseppe Zanotti heels, so I'd bet money that those were the shoes she rattled the floor with.

"What's wrong? And where is he?" I asked, even though I sensed things were a bit chaotic on the other end of the telephone receiver.

"I'm about to call the motherfucking police on his ass if he puts his hands on me again," she continued to roar.

Before I made one comment, I shook my head with disgust, because there was no doubt in my mind that she ignited this feud with my brother. Vanessa was a fucking drama queen. If the world didn't revolve around her ass, then all hell would break loose. Granted, she was gorgeous and fly. In fact, she looked like a pretty, big booty, small waist chick from Brazil. But Reggie pulled this chick straight out of one of those projects from Jersey, put her in their luxury, two-bedroom high-rise apartment, laced her with a wardrobe of high-end designers and just recently purchased her a white four door late model Jaguar with white leather interior. She was the envy of all the chicks from her old neighborhood. However, if they knew everything she had came with a price, they'd switch their focus on something else.

Unfortunately for Reggie, he and Vanessa had been together for close to four years, so he'd have to kill her to get rid of her silly ass. She came into his life when Reggie banked his first million. I'd always believed that timing was everything, so she could not have picked a better time to come into his life.

"Vanessa, put him on the phone," I instructed her because it didn't matter how mad and upset my brother was, I knew how to calm him down. It took him a few seconds to get on the line but as soon as I heard him ask me what was up, I came back with my own question. "Reggie, what is going on around there?"

"I'm about to kill this bitch! That's what's going on!" he snapped.

"Reggie, can you calm the fuck down? You got too much shit to handle tonight. So if you put your hands on Vanessa, she might just call your bluff and dial 911 on your ass this time around. And if she does that, then you won't be able to handle your affairs behind bars."

"The day she calls the police on me is the day she's getting the fuck out of here," he roared in return.

"I know that. And I'm sure she does too, but tonight isn't a good night to be testing the waters. There's a lot of money to be made before sunrise so leave that bullshit alone and get the fuck out of there," I advised him.

"I'm getting ready to leave right now," he told me.

I could tell he was moving through the house, so I was beginning to feel a little at ease. Reggie had just scored a mother load of coke. This package was the come up for the both of us. It was pure as pure can get. And the fact that we got it for a good price made our profit margin skyrocket. See, not only was I a flight attendant, I was also an opportunist. I'd only fuck with you or do something for you, if there's something in it for me. A lot of people don't like it, but that's their business. This was my life and I chose to live it the way I wanted.

Marco Chavez, who was Reggie's and mine current coke supplier, lived by this same philosophy. In the beginning, I had no idea that he was a coke dealer when I met him on one of our flights from Miami. He had the appearance of a rich real estate investor or a nightclub owner, so money was written all over him. He took my number and the rest was history. That was over a year and a half ago and even though we're no longer fucking, we still had a good working relationship, which was how I intended to keep it.

When money is involved in any situation, you have to put your feelings in your pocket and make the right choice. I learned a long time ago from both my pops and my brother that the only way a woman could survive in this world was if she didn't make decisions based on her emotions. You see men are logical, don't get into that bullshit. They come up with a plan and then they execute it. Reggie was known for taking a couple of days to make final decisions. And lately, I've adapted that same method, along with a few others.

When Reggie finally made it out to his car, I let out a sigh of relief because I knew he was about to make his move. "Do you think you're gonna need me to come out to the spot with you?" I asked him after I heard the car door close.

"Nah, I'm straight. Me and Damian will be able to handle everything," he assured me.

"Well, if you need me, just pick up the phone."

"A'ight," he said and then he hung up.

SNEAK PEEK INTO THE "NEW YORK'S FINEST PART 2: INTERNATIONALLY KNOWN"

I'M MY BROTHER'S KEEPER

It had been over three months since Damian and I had been on the run and a couple of weeks since we last spoke to Reggie. When we spoke, he acted as if he was a walking time bomb. After we hung up with him I feared that the next call we got from him would be from jail, or even worse, someone else calling to say that he'd been murdered. News like that would definitely take me over the edge for sure.

Reggie and our father, Carter Foxx, were the only two who had our phone number. Damian and I were sharing the same phone. There was no sense in either of us having separate phones. Things had changed momentarily for Damian and I. We were living in Memphis, Tennessee with his half-brother, Champ, while things chilled in New York. Compared to the city, Memphis was slow, but that might have been a good thing. It gave Damian and I time to get to really know each other. He had my back and it made me feel special. I knew I could depend on him through thick and thin. And that was definitely a good thing.

I sat outside on the balcony of a condo apartment Champ owned in downtown Memphis and began to daydream. The place overlooked the Mississippi River. It was serene, calming, and very conducive for thinking.

I thought back on the times when life was good. I had just gotten my wings to work with the airlines and soon thereafter my connections to get high potency cocaine were in full effect. Reggie was making tons of cash and I was officially apart of the high mile club. Unfortunately for us, our place at the top of the food chain was short lived. And what was so devastating about the fall from grace was that I had gotten used to the perks that came with the good life. Once you've had a taste of the good life, eating scraps wasn't appetizing at all. So while I stood outside reminiscing on the past events from my life, Damian joined me. He held out our iPhone for me to take it. "Who is it?" I uttered softly.

"It's Foxx," he replied. His tone was different and his facial expression sent me a clear message that something wasn't right. I was somewhat apprehensive about taking the phone from him, but I figured the longer I took to confront the inevitable, the longer it would take to deal with it.

After I hesitated for several seconds, I finally took the phone and said hello. "Chica, I hate to be the one to tell you this, but your brother is missing," my father said.

I wanted to act like I didn't hear him. But there was no denying what he'd just said. Realizing this, my heart sunk and my knees buckled and I was about to fall down to the floor at that moment, but Damian caught me just in time.

"Baby, watch your step," he said as he put a hand on each side of my waist.

I almost dropped the phone but Damian grabbed it before it slipped from my hand and put my father on speakerphone. “Foxx, you there?” Damian asked.

“Yeah, I’m here. Hey, listen, you two, I know this is not the best move but I’m gonna need for you guys to come back East to help me find your brother. And once we get ‘em back safely, then we can part ways.”

“Do you have any idea where he could be?” Damian pressed the issue.

“One of my sources told me he could be in the hands of Marco and his son, Miguel. But then I heard that Vanessa’s people got him because they think he had something to do with her murder.”

“Well, don’t worry about it Foxx,” Damian replied. “We’re on our way. And when we make contact, we’ll let you know.”

After Damian ended the call with my father he looked at me and said, “Let’s go. We got to head back to New York.”

I looked at Damian with a look of fear. I didn’t have a good feeling about this trip and I made him aware of it. “Damian, I’m having a really bad feeling about this,” I began to say. “I think we could be walking into a death trap if we go back.”

“But what if you’re wrong? What if it’s not a trap and he really needs us?” Damian tried to reason with me. And as much as I wanted him to be right, my feelings would not change. Reggie was a soldier at heart. He knew the streets like the back of his hands. So I felt if he was really missing, it was his choice. Reggie was the type of man that wouldn’t let anyone see him slipping or allow them to get close to him, so I found it very hard to believe that he was in harm's way. Now I may be wrong about all of this, but at that very moment, my heart rode a different wave.

Damian escorted me back into the condo and led me to the bed we shared. I took a seat at the edge of the bed and buried my face in my hand. It didn't take Damian long to lift my head back up. When he looked into my eyes, I was sure they were extremely glassy from the tears that were forming in my eyes. When I blinked, the tears started rolling down my face. Damian stood over me and tried to wipe every tear that fell from my eyes with the back of his hand.

"Stop crying baby, everything is going to be all right," he told me.

"But what if it isn't? What if we go back to New York and something bad happens?" I asked.

"If it does, just let me handle it. I promise I won't let anyone touch one hair on your head," he assured me and then he kissed me in the middle of my forehead.

I sat there and looked at him run his fingers through my hair. A few seconds later, he rubbed my back in a circular motion with the same hand. "I'll die first before I let someone do something to you," he continued as he looked into my eyes.

I remained silent in hopes that everything Damian said would resonate in my heart and my mind. I wished everything would go back the way it was before the Feds came on the scene and wreaked havoc on everything we built. Unfortunately, I was doing a bit of wishful thinking, so I snapped back into reality and decided to let Damian get in the driver's seat. Who knows, maybe he'd be able to do everything he promised? If not, in the end we'll be fucked.

Once I got my emotions back on track I got up from the bed and began to pack a few things into my luggage. I knew Damian wouldn't know how long we'd be in New York, so I took it upon myself to pack one week's worth of clothing just in case our trip was extended. Damian was on the opposite side of the bedroom gathering up his things to pack in his luggage.

"What time are we leaving?" I asked. It was at least eleven hundred miles from Memphis to New York, so I wanted to know what time we were heading out, considering the only option we had to travel was by car. We had bought something less conspicuous, a three-year-old Nissan Maxima. It had some bells and whistles: GPS navigation, CD/DVD player, and a nice sound system. But it wasn't my SUV . . . I really missed driving around the city in my whip.

Damian looked down at his wristwatch. "I wanna get out of here within the next hour," he replied.

It was eleven-thirty in the morning and it was very sunny outside. The temperature had to have been around seventy-five degrees because of the constant breeze I felt when it hit my face. It seemed like the perfect day to travel but when you think about where we had to travel to, the thought alone changed the mood and sent a dark cloud over my head.

"Do you think it would be a good idea for us to drive across country in broad daylight? I mean, we are gonna have to make a couple of stops to get gas and food along the way," I began to explain. Since we had been in Memphis, we had been low-key, chilling out mostly at home. I had cut my hair lower and had been wearing different color wigs. Hell, in Memphis no one paid us any attention besides the occasional old woman or couple telling us how cute we looked as a couple. Plus we had been sporting a lot of sunshades and just that simple accessory alone changed out appearance.

"We own sunshades, right?" he asked.

"Yeah."

"Well, there you go. And besides, no one knows our car and we have new IDs, so we're going to be just fine."

I sighed, "I know I'm being more paranoid than usual. It's just that things have been good since we've been here and I just don't want anything to mess it up." Although Champ was a straight up guy, he knew people with street creds and was able to hook up with a cat who was an underground expert at doing fake IDs. We had passports, new driver's licenses and social security cards.

"It's normal to feel the way you're feeling right now," Damian tried reassuring me. "But at the same time I want you to know that I'm gonna be with you and I will die first before I let something happen to you."

I looked into Damian's eyes and body movements while he poured his heart out to me and he made it perfectly clear about how much he loved me. I needed to hear the sincerity in his voice and he gave it to me. Growing up as a daddy's girl and the baby of the family with Reggie being the oldest, I'd always been sheltered and protected. No one ever had a chance to mess with me as long as my family was around. So, to have Damian around to fill those shoes while my father and Reggie were absent, definitely filled the void.

After Damian and I packed up our things he got on the phone and called his brother, Champ, to let him know of our plans to leave. He didn't go into any details about where we were going, but he did tell him about how long we'd be gone. Immediately after Damian ended their call he grabbed his 9mm Glock from his sock drawer, his sunshades and car keys, and headed to the front door. I followed in his footsteps after I grabbed my handbag and my sunshades.

The moment I stepped foot outside the front door, anxiety hit me squarely in the face. My stomach started rumbling and fear instantly consumed me to the point that I stopped in my tracks. I stood there at the front door like a statue with my handbag across my shoulders and my luggage in one hand.

Damian turned around when he noticed that I wasn't behind him and said, "Babe, what's wrong? Are you okay?"

"I'm scared, Damian," I told him.

Damian put his things in the car and then he walked back to where I was standing. "I told you, I got you, right?"

"Yes," I said, barely audible.

"Well, then, let's go," he said, and then he took my luggage from my hand and grabbed my other hand and escorted me to the car.

New York, here we come . . .

Coming April 2013